Kim Pees, Sheryl Flees, and Mary Buys a Blender

Matt Godwin

Copyright © 2020 Matt Godwin

All rights reserved

The characters and events portrayed in this book are fictitious. Any similarity to real persons, living or dead, is coincidental and not intended by the author.

No part of this book may be reproduced, or stored in a retrieval system, or transmitted in any form or by any means, electronic, mechanical, photocopying, recording, or otherwise, without express written permission of the publisher.

ISBN: 9798652740375

Printed in the United States of America

To my wife, Jaime

Chapter 1

Tom Meets Arthur, Arthur Meets Mary

Mary's shaved armpits are beginning to test the strength of his sister's medical-grade antiperspirant. He wonders if the carpet is clean. He also wonders what faint bodily odor he is picking up beneath the new-appliance smell wafting off the ass-prolapsing war crime of a sex toy before him.

Mary doesn't think it will fit in his butt, at least not without murdering his plumbing. This situation isn't what he had pictured when he agreed to meet this guy. On the app, Tom had told Arthur to call him Mary. He had also told him, *treat me like you don't respect me*.

Twenty minutes ago, Mary was in his sister Gwen's car at a stoplight, touching up his shave job with a razor she kept in her glove compartment. He wanted his legs to be silky smooth for this guy. Gwen dropped it out the window a few minutes after she drove away. *Ew,* she thought.

Arthur's hairy foot pushes Mary's face into the carpet. Mary's knees are tender from being dragged across it. He is looking at the ominous object placed a few inches from his nose. The silicone dick is hefty enough to club a horse. *Fuck that.*

The living room is exactly what you would expect to be in a suburban house in Palm Beach County, Florida. The leather sofa is still not as comfortable as the floor model had been. A plate caked in dried tomato sauce sits next to perspiring drinking glasses on a coffee table from the same place as the shitty sofa.

The television is too big for the cabinet supporting it. Arthur's wife bought it online years ago. The TV wasn't the only thing that was smaller back then. Arthur looks approvingly at his reflection in its big unlit screen. Dominating this skinny little slut is making him feel powerful.

Mary is wondering if the rubbery ogre cock belongs to Arthur's wife or if he reserves this for the wayward young crossdressers he meets online. He had said in his texts that his wife was in New York, visiting family with the kids for the week.

Mary wants real dick. The glossy black obelisk looming down at him is a caricature of cock at best. The fake veins look cartoony. The head is stippled in a way that gives the impression of skin rather than imitating it. Its studded balls stick straight out above an oversized suction cup at its base.

Who else has Arthur introduced his rubbery friend to? Maybe his own butt? No, he said his butthole was like Fort Knox when Mary had asked him if he liked anal play in their text messages.

"Suck it," Arthur commands as he peels the sticky bottom of his foot from Mary's reddened cheek.

Maybe he just wants to watch me drool on it for a bit, Mary thinks to himself. *Okay, get into character. I'm just some slut a married man wants to humiliate.* He tries to be sexy as he obediently crawls closer and pokes the tip of it with his tongue.

"That's it, Mary. Daddy wants his baby girl to slurp."

"Mmmkay, Daddy."

"Don't talk! Your voice makes this feel gay," Arthur barks, sounding irritated.

Yikes, what a jerk, Mary thinks, feeling stung by the remark. He looks up at Arthur with a pouty face. Arthur smacks the expression from Mary's face. He crouches down, putting his hand between Mary's pink pigtails, and shoves. Mary's lips slide over the unreasonably huge rubbery black dick head.

Mary's jaw pops. He feels assaulted, but when he gets a whiff of this corny dad's rapey locker-room cologne, something shifts beneath his polka-dotted skirt: His stiffening penis is forcing its way free of the bright green thong apprehending it. *What the fuck is wrong with me?* he wonders (and not for the first time).

Arthur's face is red with adrenaline and lust. He's rubbing himself through his horrible khaki cargo shorts, with an idiot-grin on his face. Mary pulls his head back and noses at the stiff fabric of Arthur's crotch. *Hint, hint. Gimme the real thing, you big dope...*

Arthur slaps the back of Mary's thigh and shoves his head back down, saying, "I said slurp, baby. Show Daddy how much you like to suck." Mary obeys, leaning in to slobber. He gives up trying to fit the whole head in his mouth. *Not gonna happen.* He starts licking down the shaft instead, stopping at the balls to suck noisily.

"Yeah, like that. You're a dirty little bitch."

Mary can't help it. For some reason, being degraded by this abrasive shithead is making him want to cum dumpster-sized quantities of sperm all over this house.

He feels a hand around his throat, pulling his head pulled back roughly. A lubey hand slides up his skirt and struggles to gain purchase on his thong. Arthur lets go of Mary's neck and forces a thumb into his mouth.

"Suck, bitch."

Mary drools on Arthur's thumb but freezes as the man brutally yanks his thong taut, flossing him between his girly testicles. His legs instinctively clamp shut to protect his sack from further abuse.

"What's wrong, feeling shy? A modest little slut. I like that."

The stretchy fabric of the thong finally tears. Mary feels a wash of relief as his nuts fall free. One of the lube-slick fingers forces itself inside his tediously manicured butthole. *Well, like the old saying goes, if you keep a tidy house, you're probably expecting guests.* Mary fails to suppress a nervous laugh at this bit of inner monologue.

"Oh, you think this funny, you awkward little twat?"

Another finger is forced inside him, stretching his pink butthole. Mary sucks on Arthur's salty thumb as a third finger slides inside of him. Learning to wax and bleach his butthole had taken sustained effort; he is always happy to put it to use.

Mary backs up onto Arthur's fingers and wiggles. Having this pleb's hammy digits explore his insides, stretching open his food-grade aseptic anus, feels cathartic. It feels *right*.

But just as he is starting to enjoy the abuse, his abuser stops fingering and says, "I want beer."

"Do you have any?" Mary asks in Tom's voice by accident.

Smack

Mary receives a hard slap on the cheek from the hand that had been thumb-fucking his mouth. His burning cheek is slick with saliva from Arthur's thumb.

"I said don't talk, you little bitch," Arthur snaps at him angrily. He belches a little and smacks his chest for some reason. *Heartburn?* "Of course I have beer, but I have to warn you. I am one *mean* fucking drunk," he laughs at this candid confession.

Chapter 2

Arthur Walks His Dog Mary

"Stay here, slut." Arthur gets up and goes into the bedroom.

The AC in this place is so much better than ours, thinks Mary. *Wait, why did he go into the bedroom if he wanted beer? Wouldn't that be in the fridge? This fucking guy is a mess.*

Mary waits patiently with a burning cheek and a torn thong dangling under his skirt. The saliva on his face has all but dried. The lube on his butthole feels chilly. Goosebumps cover his skinny white body.

Arthur reenters the room with a disturbing grin on his flakey sunburned face. In one hand is a choke chain fit for a pit bull and in the other is a… *what the fuck? Is that a board game?*

Mary figures the chain is for him. He starts getting hard again as he imagines getting choked with it. *But why the board game? One minute this guy is talking about beer and slapping me around, the next minute he grabs a fucking board game like he wants to spend some quality time with auntie.*

Arthur sets the box on the table and kneels next to Mary. He strokes the exposed skin between Mary's tacky sequined tube top and the waistline of his skirt. Mary leans into his affection.

"Good girl. That's a *good* girl. Daddy loves his girl because she behaves so well," Arthur says as he slips the choke chain around Mary's slender neck. The metal links are cold against his skin. His stiffening penis dangles between his legs like the tail of a submissive puppy.

"Good girl, Mary. Want Daddy to take his good girl for a walk?"

Mary shifts into a kneeling position, bringing his hands up to his chest in a show of canine acquiescence. Roleplaying as Arthur's dog feels dangerously close to furry play, but he's getting off on it despite his reservations about that particular subculture. *Calm down, Mary, you're not wearing a fucking pluto costume, and this isn't Seattle,* he reassures himself.

He nods eagerly at his simple-minded owner. Arthur grins stupidly and scratches Mary behind the ear. Mary lets his tongue hang out and breathes heavily. Arthur pushes two fingers, still sticky with lube, into Mary's mouth. Mary sucks them down to the knuckle, batting his long black lashes, trying his best to look seductive. Arthur pulls them out and wipes them in Mary's hair. He tugs the leash.

He walks a shamelessly crawling dog-Mary into the kitchen. The tile floor is cold on Mary's rug-burned knees. Arthur stops Mary in front of the fridge.

"Be a good little bitch and get Daddy a six-pack."

Dog-Mary nudges the door open with his snout and retrieves the six-pack of cans by biting the plastic and pulling them from the fridge with his teeth.

Craft beer? Of course, it's craft beer. Bet this fucking stooge feels edgy buying this beardo shitwater. Mary wonders what time it is.

"Good girl. Now bring Daddy's beer back to the sofa, and maybe he will share."

Uh, nah, bro, that's okay — more for you.

Chapter 3

Tom's Childhood Friend

When Tom (aka Mary) was seven years old, a family moved into a neighboring townhouse. He was wandering around the parking lot the day they moved in. Aiden's mother and father were carrying a sofa down the ramp of a moving truck. Tom asked them if they needed help. They laughed and said no, and thanked him in a way that he thought sounded condescending.

Their son Aiden walked out of the house complaining about the size of his room. Tom interrupted him by formally introducing himself to the boy, hand extended (as seen on TV). Aiden's mom smiled and suggested they have a "playdate" once they were all settled. "Maybe Aiden can show you his video games," the woman suggested.

Aiden's games were all single-player, probably because he was an only child. Tom's parents were divorced. Something about seeing two spouses get along made Tom resent them.

Aiden was the kind of kid that wanted to show off his stuff but wasn't keen on sharing any of it. Tom thought Aiden was spoiled. He judged him for having a room full of toys and happy parents that ate dinner with him.

Tom spent a lot of time at Aiden's that summer. Even though he didn't like the kid, it was still better than being alone.

Being alone in his townhouse made him anxious. The silence haunted him. He would notice how quiet it was, and the stillness would grow into something suffocating. That summer, Aiden's house served as a quick way out from beneath the heaviness of all that quiet.

Sitting next to Aiden while he played games soon failed to hold his attention. He devised other ways of entertaining himself, like socially experimenting on Aiden's mom.

At first, she ate it up. She talked about Tom excessively to her husband at the dinner table. *What a bright kid,* she would say.

It was a pretty simple trick. Tom would walk into the kitchen or the family room, wherever he happened to find her, and ask her an innocent question to get a conversation going. He would listen to her answer with his head tilted, nodding, and smiling – absorbing her every word.

Then, a few days later, he would bring up something trivial she had said. This simple act made a big impression – a child listening to her, really hearing her. She loved her husband and her son, but they *never* listened to her like Tom did.

It was Tom's other little game that would eventually get someone killed.

He thought of it as "opposite stealing." It started as an impulsive thing, mostly free of malice or intention – just childish mischief. That changed quickly.

He would take something he found poking around their neighborhood and then place it somewhere in their house when no one was looking. His first experiment had been an empty wine bottle underneath the sink in the master bathroom.

Aiden's mother discovered the wine bottle when she was retrieving a replacement toothbrush from a bulk pack. She didn't drink alcohol, but she knew her husband liked to have a beer or two just to fit in with his golf buddies.

She had never griped about him drinking or told him he couldn't do it. She appreciated that he didn't drink regularly, but she wouldn't have hassled him if he wanted to enjoy some wine in his own home. He was the patriarch and breadwinner of their traditional Christian household. She was willingly subservient to him out of religious obedience. As far as she was concerned, he could do as he darn-well pleased. *Why did he try to hide this under the sink? What was he ashamed of?*

Tom paid close attention. He wanted to see what would happen when someone found it. A couple of days later, there were subtle but detectable changes in the mood of the house. He knew he had caused something to shift. He noticed how the woman's nonchalance had given way to persistent moodiness. Her brow furrowed more often. He saw her stop in the middle of doing things and just stare into space.

He felt drunk on power, knowing this was probably due to his chaotic interference. He decided to "opposite steal" something else.

He grew addicted to watching the seeds he planted flower into marital tension. He fed on the woman's anxiety.

Chapter 4

A Brief Check-In with Arthur and Mary

Arthur leans forward and slides the six-pack and the board game to his side of the table. He cracks open one of the cans, takes a long drink, belches and grunts with satisfaction.

"Oh, that?" he sees Mary looking at the box on the table, "Your fuck face is gonna be my new little fuck hole."

Everything that comes out of this turd's mouth is a groundbreaking revelation of lobotomite poetry, Mary observes.

The box features a wacky picture of a wild-eyed kid with an O-shaped piece of plastic holding his mouth open like he's at the dentist's office. He appears to be trying to read something from a card while his family laughs uncontrollably at his plastic-impeded speech.

Gross. So, this guy wants to use his kid's innocent game on his kinky internet lover instead of buying a proper O-ring? Didn't they sell O-rings at whatever seedy-ass porn store you bought that giant ass-ram you made me suck? Cheapass motherfucker. Torture me with the good shit. I don't want to put some diseased child's dirty-ass plastic game piece in my mouth.

Mary fights to regain control of his thoughts before his wandering mind incites enough loathing to sabotage his exciting afternoon of dangerous sex with someone's perverted dad. *Stop it, slut. At least you're not bored. Get into character. You are an object. You are here to be enjoyed and then thrown away like trash. You don't make the rules.* Mary's mind chastises itself with dirty talk to re-establish the mood.

Chapter 5

Young Tom's Evil Plan

It was nearing the end of summer. Tom had managed to deteriorate the happiness of his neighbor's family significantly. Aiden's mother no longer seemed to take pleasure in his attentive conversation. At first, she seemed distracted. She would still talk to him, but it was clear her mind was busy running through possible scenarios that might explain the things she kept finding in her house – like a shower cap stained with hair dye in the kitchen trash can. *Who the frick was dying their hair in our house?*

Her husband Cory worked a lot. She respected him for this. She thought of a strong work ethic as a rare and wholesome quality, characteristic of a God-fearing man. She didn't mind his long absences. He spent most weekends at home, which allowed her to pursue her calling.

She spent many a weekend working to influence positive change in their community. She participated in phone campaigns at church to pressure local politicians about things like prayer in school, installing security cameras at local parks, funding anti-drug initiatives. She and the other ladies often passed out flyers at public events. She helped circulate petitions among fellow congregation members.

She had always felt like a decent person with a full life, but now she worried that she had somehow neglected her husband's needs. Why would strange women be dying their hair in her house? What was driving her man to drink?

Tom spied on Sheryl as she wrestled with these thoughts.

When Tom's parents had split up, his sister opted to go live with their dad. The two of them didn't even visit anymore. He felt like he and his mom depressed them or something. His mom worked multiple jobs just to keep up with the bills. He hardly ever saw the woman.

Tom had already watched more movies than most people watch in a lifetime. Late-night entertainment painted a dark picture of the world for Tom. He saw people murder people for money. He saw men rape and abuse women despite their tearful protests.

The sexual indulgences of ungratified spouses were the stuff of gripping late-night drama. *Secrets destroy marriages.*

He was a lonely child in a confusing world. Pranking Sheryl had given him his first taste of power. He had taken what he couldn't have (a happy home with two loving parents) and caused it to wither by the work of his small hand. What had started as a thoughtless diversion quickly fermented into a dark and serious plan.

He would try to cause Aiden's parents to get divorced. Then, conveniently, he would be emotionally available for Aiden's mother during what would doubtlessly be a difficult time for her. In movies, there was often a charming gentleman character who provided the brokenhearted damsel with a shoulder to cry on. He would be that charming gentleman.

Then, in her vulnerable state, she would fall passionately in love with him. He would let this happen for just long enough to collect irrefutable evidence that she was a child predator. Then he would call the police.

Her lawyer would recommend bribing him with a massive sum of money. He would accept, and they would settle out of court, like the people he saw on the news.

With all that money, his mother wouldn't need to work anymore. They would be able to afford video games like Aiden's, except the two-player kind. Maybe his dad and sister would even start coming around again. They would want to play too, and he would happily share, unlike Aiden. *That selfish fuckhead.*

Chapter 6

Mary Spills Some Beer

"You thirsty, slut?"

Mary kneels obediently on the floor at the edge of the sofa. Arthur pulls on the choke chain. Mary's mouth is held open by the family-friendly plastic O-ring from Arthur's board game. Much to Mary's relief, it tastes like dish soap and not Pop-Tart slime or whatever kids eat these days.

Having his mouth forced open and kneeling at this pervy everyman's hairy feet makes him feel like a public toilet, like a hussied up semen urinal. He doesn't know how much of this is roleplaying. A queasy feeling that he may be in real danger is making the experience believable. He finds himself melting into his submissive role with minimal effort. *This guy could probably force him to do anything he wanted.*

Knees on the carpet, a chain dog leash around his neck, saliva dripping from the O-shaped lipstick ring of his mouth – waiting to find out if Arthur is kinky or cruel has his cock harder than a socket wrench. Mary daydreams about this sort of shit. He feels like a plucked flower – beautiful, delicate, and doomed.

Mary follows his dim-bulb host's eyes to the abandoned dinner plate on the coffee table. The man picks up the knife lying across the dry remnants of *what, chicken parm?*

Arthur pulls the chain taut, dragging Mary between his legs. He pushes Mary's head back with a rough palm against his forehead. Mary looks up at him with a mixture of pleading and arousal. He tries to look more seductive than concerned, but his heart is pounding. Arthur puts the dull tip of the food-crusted knife against Mary's cheek.

"I asked you a question, bitch. What, are you dumb?"

Mary tries to say yes, he is thirsty, but the plastic apparatus forcing his mouth open makes it impossible, so he just nods.

"Ah, so you *are* dumb. Well, at least you *know* you're dumb. Figures if you know you're dumb, you know *something*, so you can't be dumb as all that..."

Ah, the old gym class bully switcheroo technique. Mary bitterly recalls this particular species of degenerate humor from his days in the public school system. *Does it feel good when you masturbate? No? Ah, so you do masturbate!*

Despite his overwhelming feelings of superiority towards this beefy beer-drinking lout, the arousal he feels being degraded by him is fucking real. *I need a therapist.*

"Here, you dumb bitch. Drink. You deserve it for knowing your place."

Arthur pours beer into Mary's perfectly circular face opening. Mary tries to swallow with his mouth open, but some of the trendy bro beer takes the wrong route. Mary coughs beer foam down the front of his prostitute costume and onto the carpet.

"What the fuck?! I try to share my nice cold beer, and you *ruin* my carpet. What kind of thanks is that? You want my wife to think she's married to a slob?" Arthur hits Mary in the face repeatedly, knocking the plastic O-ring out of Mary's mouth.

Mascara-tinted tears paint Mary's face. He isn't sad. He's just shaken up from being slapped.

Arthur grabs Mary's pink pigtails and shoves his streaked face into the beer saturated carpet.

"Suck it clean, or I'm gonna fuck you up, bitch."

Mary, now shivering from being soaked with novelty beer in a freezing house, sucks at the carpet with visible effort. *Is this guy genuinely mad about his carpet, or is he just getting into this shit?* Mary wonders as he imitates a wet-vac.

"Might as well suck these while you're down there," Arthur says, jamming a toe into Mary's mouth. *So, that's what sandal-smell tastes like*, Mary thinks. He goes ham on the toe in a sex-charged pageant of vulnerability and redemption.

Chapter 7

Speaking of Toes

Aiden's mom felt her heart drop into her stomach with an acidy splash as she looked down in horror at her latest discovery.

The wine, the shower cap, the receipt, the earing – finding evidence of a possible affair was one thing, severed body parts were another.

The leftover meatloaf she had eaten started having claustrophobic thoughts. Her throat tightened. Her mouth tasted like bile.

It was just lying there on the floor next to her husband's nightstand. There were several curly black hairs just above the knuckle. It was man's toe with a sparkly cerulean-blue toenail.

She looked at the toe. The toe looked at her. The meatloaf looked at her esophageal sphincter.

Hoping it wasn't real, she picked it up and gave it a tentative sniff. A yellow jet of vomit launched from the mouth of her now colorless face. Chunks of lunch rained down with a splash on the nightstand, on the oak patterned laminate, on the toe in her hand.

Chapter 8

Mary Puts in That Work

Mary sucks off each of Arthurs's calloused toes. He is very thorough. Anything to prevent Arthur from remembering the monstrous dildo they abandoned by the TV. Mary put a lot of work into getting his asshole to look like they do in porn, but that thing is way bigger than a porno dick. It's designed to harm.

Arthur sits up, freeing his foot from Mary's mouth. He chugs the rest of his beer, burps heartily, and reaches for another. He looks as though he is about to stand. *Uh oh*. Mary slithers between Arthur's legs and breathes hot hair through the crotch of his khaki dad-shorts. Mary figures if he can get Arthur to cum by blowing him, the guy will lose interest in trying to store his silicone murder appendage in Mary's Jim-locker. Also, he kind of feels like sucking dick.

Arthur looks vulnerable somehow. Getting head isn't as empowering as porn likes to depict it. The giver takes the receiver's most sensitive and cherished body part into their mouth – a cavity optimized by evolution to separate meat from bone, to turn eggplant into digestible mush, to crack a nut's shell and mash it into pulp.

At first, Arthur is hesitant about this unprompted change in their power dynamic, but he isn't about to say no to fucking a warm and inviting face-hole. He looks down at the runny-eyed girlboy exhaling into his crotch with a hot lipstick-smeared mouth. Mary looks like an off-brand hooker. Arthur gives in.

Mary unfastens Arthur's woven leather belt, unbuttons his shorts, bites the tab of his fly, and pulls it down with his teeth. Mary can see hairy cock skin through the window of Arthur's plaid big-pack boxers. He licks it. Arthur grunts.

Mary fishes Arthur's dick out – average but not unattractive. Mary had suspected Arthur's aggressive attitude might be a symptom of genital inadequacy, but the man's dick is just fine. Mary bats it from side to side with a pink tongue, feeling like he's maneuvering a salty joystick. Arthur is wearing a satisfied smirk that says he's probably thinking a bunch of sentences that make use of the word "daddy" and "bitch."

Arthur puts his meaty right hand on the back of Mary's head and pulls it down. His slippery dick head rubs against the back wall of Mary's mouth and slides down into an unprotesting throat, challenging a gag reflex that was born to be a quitter. He holds Mary's head down, humping into it mercilessly. Mary practices nasal breathing while enduring this brutal oral plumbing.

Arthur gets tired of pumping and lays back, giving Mary the reigns. Having the benefit of knowing what feels good is an asset to Mary's headgame – he works both hands, twisting, putting some elbow grease into this shit, occasionally releasing his grip to go full-keto on the meat. Mary is the auto-hammer of cock sucking – slurping, sucking, swallowing, jerking with a performative flair charged by a true passion for service.

Arthur turns on the TV, takes his shirt off, and leans over Mary to get yet another beer, pressing his sweating potbelly against Mary's forehead. Mary picks a pubic hair off of his tongue and resumes sucking. Arthur cracks the beer and follows a lengthy swallow with a theatrical sigh of contentedness.

Chapter 9

Aiden's Mom Suspects Tom

Sheryl was alone in the bedroom, standing by where she found the toe the previous day. Her disgust had since turned to anger. She had placed the offending digit in a baggie and hidden it. *Cory is going to explain himself, and then I am going to make it crystal clear that whatever twisted secret life he is living is officially over. No more secrets. No more little surprises. No more frickin' toes.*

If her husband got himself arrested, she and Aiden would be destitute. She couldn't imagine trying to hack it out there in the filthy world without her husband, her rock.

Her husband was putting his family in jeopardy. *How could he?* She just couldn't wrap her head around it. *Why does he suddenly want to drag his own family to hell? It doesn't make any frigging sense. The man is a Christian!*

She had seen him moved by the word during many a sermon in church. She had seen his righteous tears with her own eyes.

Cory works hard. He loves his kid. He loves me. Sure, he enjoys an occasional round of golf with his friends, but he never burdens me by bringing them around. Also, a wrapper from a cigarette pack just sitting there in a dish... really? The man has never smoked a cigarette in his life. The receipt in his pocket was for sushi! He hates sushi.

Smoking, secretly drinking, helping strange woman dye their hair, eating Unagi rolls, leaving severed toes lying around the bedroom – none of these behaviors were compatible with the man she married.

Then it hit her. This was all just some elaborate prank. A chill ran down her spine. *That fuc... frickin kid. It had to be. Who else could it be?* There was just no way that she had unknowingly married the kind of monster that would be secretly running around on his wife, eating eel with purple-haired women, and carrying a severed toe in his pocket like a good luck charm. She couldn't even picture Cory with a cigarette in his well-bred mouth.

It couldn't be Aiden either, bless his heart; the boy was a simpleton. He was as sheltered and fragile as they come. Besides, he was too busy staring at the screen.

It had to be Tom. *That little sociopath has been f-f-fricking with me all along!*

Chapter 10

Young Tom Goes for a Car Ride

The golf course was within walking distance from Tom's community. It was a Par 3 course, a place for aging men to day-drink outdoors with their buddies under the guise of casual weekend sporting.

Tom stood in the parking lot, a lonely kid with a lost expression on his face. He was just bored, searching the pavement for noteworthy litter. Aiden had once complained to him about being dragged there by his dad. Cory had tried to teach his boy to swing a club. Tom wished *his* dad would try to teach him things. He certainly wouldn't do any complaining about it.

He felt nothing but curiosity when the big Buick pulled up next to him and rolled down its window.

"What's your name?" asked the stranger in the car. His breath smelled like a recycling bin. He had fragments of potato chip lodged in the hairs of his mustache.

"Tom."

"Are you okay, Tom? You look lost." The stranger's voice was sweet in a way that sounded fake.

"I'm not lost. I walked here. I should go home," Tom said, trying to hint that he had no interest in talking to this sweaty rube.

"You walked? It's too hot outside for that. Where do you live, Tom?"

The guy reminded Tom of the bad guys in the type of movies where some rugged dad has to track down his abducted kid, saying a bunch of badass shit and busting people's heads open in the process. Those movies had taught Tom a valuable lesson: Even aging bald guys can roundhouse kick people if they get mad enough.

"I live down the street in one of those townhouses," Tom responded with feigned naivety, deciding to fuck with the guy. "Where do *you* live, mister?" he threw in the word 'mister' just to hear himself say it out loud.

"Please, call me Greg. I live in a mansion, Tom!"

"COOL!" Tom responded, imitating the man's feigned excitement in a way he hoped would come across as childlike wonder.

"My son has his very own water park in our back yard. Would you like to meet him?"

"I don't know, mister…" Tom added a layer of hesitation, playing the role of boy-victim in the PSA that this goon seemed intent on acting out.

"It's Greg, little buddy, call me Greg."

"I don't know, Greg. I guess that sounds fun."

"Hop in, little man," Greg reached across to the passenger-side door and opened it for Tom to get in. Greg was fat.

"Nice car, Greg," Tom said once he had strapped himself in with the seatbelt.

"Thanks, little bud. What kind of music do you like?"

"Rap," Tom said honestly. He could tell this was the wrong answer by the look on Greg's face.

"You're kidding! What about rock and roll music, baby? Have you ever heard Rod Steward?" Greg asked, trying and failing to salvage an awkward moment. The name sounded more like a job description than a name to Tom. He imagined someone in a denim jumper guiding a metal pole into an industrial-looking machine.

"Sure, Greg. Let's listen to Rod."

"Attaboy, Tom. Rock music is man's music," Greg said, giving Tom a pretend punch on the shoulder. He pushed play on the console, and music came on. Tom was legitimately impressed. The speakers were worlds apart from the tinny buzzing cans in his mom's car.

Some husky-voiced adult was asking the listener, "Do you think I'm sexy?" to musical accompaniment that sounded strangely urgent to Tom. He didn't hate it.

After a few minutes of driving, Greg stopped the car at the backdoor of a restaurant in a strip mall. Tom was more curious than shocked. He knew this pudgy dill hole was bad news from the moment he heard him deliver his shady-ass 'I live in a mansion' bit. This dirty clown didn't live in a mansion. Tom had only come along out of a virgin cocktail of apathy and boredom. He had never been abducted before, and he wanted to see where the adventure would lead.

"Hey Tom, I have a great idea!" said Greg sounding a little crazy. *I fucking bet you do,* thought Tom. "Have you ever seen the kitchen of a restaurant?" Greg asked, not waiting for Tom to answer before adding, "This isn't just any restaurant. This restaurant is special!"

"Why is it special?" Tom asked.

"Because I own it, little Bud. Let's go inside. I'll make us both lunch! How does that sound?"

It sounds like you're more fucked up than I thought you were when I got in your car, you chubby worm fart, thought Tom with a grin before responding, "That sounds great. I'm starving!"

Greg looked in his review mirror for a minute before they got out of the car. He located the key to the restaurant among his numerous keys. When they were inside, Tom heard Greg slide a lock at the top of the door before he turned the lights on. *Hmm, that's not good.*

"How about some nice hot soup, pal? We make some killer minestrone," Greg didn't notice the pun.

"I like soup, but do you think I could have a sandwich too?" Tom asked, figuring this creep would probably accommodate him. Tom wasn't stupid enough to consume a bowl of hot liquid from a predatory stranger, but he thought it would be pretty hard to hide anything in a sandwich. His mom did her best to keep food in the house, but he would probably be eating cereal for dinner again while she pulled a night shift. A sandwich sounded better than a bowl of cartoon-endorsed diabetes.

"Uh, I think we can arrange that, little man," Greg said. He suggested Tom find them a table.

The restaurant was creepy. Stick-on imitation stained glass covered the windows. Even after Tom found the light switch to the dining area, the place looked gloomy. Framed black and white photos of people Tom didn't recognize lined the walls. Dust crowned the pendant-style light fixtures.

He walked up to the old-timey jukebox and punched random buttons until music came on. A tragic sounding boyish voice sang, "I fall in love too easily..." The singing gave way to heart-wrenching sighs of melodic despair from a flawlessly played trumpet. A piano trickled in a string of fragile notes somewhere in the background. For a moment, Tom felt like crying. He'd never heard this song before. It sounded like the jazz they played in grainy old movies but without any of the joy.

Tom's instincts told him that he should probably give his present circumstances some thought. Greg was still in the kitchen. *Drugging the damn soup*, Tom thought. *I wonder if he has a gun? Shit, I don't have a gun. I don't even know kung fu. This could get uncomfortable.*

He tried the front door to the restaurant. Predictably, it was locked from inside by a redundant collection of deadbolts hidden behind decorative red fabric. He looked at the windows, thinking he might be able to chuck a chair through one, but it was clear from the shadows cast on the fake stained-glass that they had bars over them.

He looked around the restaurant, wondering what the kid from *Home Alone* would do in this situation. Tom collected olive oil bottles from the tables on his way to the bar by the entrance of the kitchen. He set them on the cushion of a bar stool and unscrewed their caps. One by one, he emptied their contents onto the tile floor. It smelled delicious.

Chapter 11

Mary Gets a Facial

A basketball game plays on the massive TV. Arthur finishes yet another beer. Mary feels like he has been sucking on the guy's dingus for a long time. If someone had blown him like he was blowing Arthur, he would have busted a while ago.

Arthur starts breathing heavier. His hips rise to meet the bobbing of Mary's head. Mary makes that *glop glop glop* sound porn stars make in videos where the camera lens gets all slimy.

"Fuckkkkk," Arthur exclaims as he pulls his dick out of Mary's mouth and super-soaks his girly face with a relentless torrent of pearly jizz. He lays back on the sofa with a sigh and shoves Mary away with his recently spit-shined foot.

Mary falls back on his rump. He sits cross-legged a couple of feet from the coffee table. His face is dripping with a muddy sludge of semen, saliva, mascara, and lipstick. His erection pokes up from beneath his disheveled skirt like it's about to make a boy scout's oath. Mary looks at the deflating heap of a man on the sofa through a translucent curtain of magic baby batter.

"You look like shit," Arthur tells Mary as he tilts more beer into his mouth, "I have to piss." He gets up with a wobble. A look of concentration forms on his bleary face. *The ape has had a thought*, Mary observes. A drop of migrating cum falls from his chin onto the rigid head of his prick and rolls down its shaft.

"Here, I'm going to help you get cleaned up," Arthur says as he walks into the kitchen, swaying. *Such tenderness*, Mary thinks with suspicion.

Arthur comes back into the living room with a roll of black plastic trash bags. He kicks aside the dildo to make room on the floor in front of the coffee table. *At least I won't have a flabby prolapsed colon when I leave this fuckball's shitty house,* Mary thinks with relief when he looks at the discarded silicone demon-peen that Arthur dismissed with his foot.

Arthur doesn't bother picking up Mary's choke chain and going through the theatrics of domination. Mary would have preferred a little more of that, but it's obvious this wet brain is no longer aroused enough to help Mary cum. He just points at the trash bags he laid out to protect the carpet and tells him to kneel there.

Oh, I get it. He wants to piss on me, Mary realizes.

Mary crawls over to the trash bags and kneels, looking up expectantly through a membrane of sex fluids and east coast drugstore cosmetics. Gritty though it may be, he likes where this is going. He has never had cum pissed off of his face before.

Chapter 12

Young Tom Eats a Sandwich

Light from the kitchen reflected in the dark pool of extra virgin bread moistener. Tom gazed approvingly at the lake of oil he had made on the floor.

The dark and beautiful trumpet song ended. Tom recognized the next song from frozen pasta commercials. Something about Chicago. *Blah*, thought Tom. He walked back over to the jukebox.

He reached up and punched buttons at random again. He wanted some Wayne. Something with 808s and stick talk. He liked songs about money. He liked repetition. He especially liked when female rappers spent sixteen bars talking about their genitals in a tone of voice that made them seem more scary than appealing.

The record changed just as he heard Greg exited the kitchen. The song sounded fucking ancient. Some guy started chanting the words "return to sender" with a bouncy sounding saxophone farting out a little hype between the lines.

Greg shouted, "Heck yeah, I love Elvis!" as he entered with a tray of hot soup and sandwiches. Tom turned just in time to watch him slip on the olive oil. He collapsed in a noisy chaos of boiling-hot soup, salami sandwiches, and shattered dishware. His head made an audible crack as it hit the tile. Drugged minestrone and cutlery showered down on his face – a serrated dinner knife flipping in the air like a leotarded pedo-bait prodigy doing some Olympics bullshit for her rich ass parents and then fell point-first into his eye socket. It stuck out of his popped eyeball like the flag on Iwo Jima. Blood pooled around his cracked head, making organic patterns in the olive oil.

Tom stood over the body with wide eyes. The scene was pretty grim. *This is just like TV,* Tom thought. Elvis was still boopy-dooping "return to sender" from the dining area.

Tom looked over at the bar and noticed all the bottles of liquor. He hopped over the spreading lake of fluids, unscrewed the cap on a green bottle, and sniffed. The contents made his eyes water, but he'd seen so many badass movie characters standing around all cocky with the shit that he knew it wouldn't kill him. He took a tentative sip. *Dang, this stuff is harsh.*

"You want some, Greg?" He offered the bottle to his abductor's motionless body. He grimaced through another tentative sip and coughed. *Yeah, no thanks,* he thought and put the bottle back. He needed something to get the taste out of his mouth.

He looked back at Greg. A mostly intact salami sandwich sat invitingly on Greg's ghostless chest.

Not wanting to get oil or blood on his sneakers, he walked across Greg's dead arm like a balance beam and hopped onto his fat legs. Greg was like a makeshift man-raft on an ocean of gore-flavored salad dressing.

Tom picked up the sandwich and took a bite. He was hungry. The salami was a little dry, but the bread was surprisingly good. *Maybe mom will take me here for dinner sometime.*

When he finished, he snatched the key-ring from Greg's pocket and hopped off the corpse into the kitchen.

He found Greg's cell phone between an orange prescription bottle and a mortar and pestle. He pressed a button. The screen illuminated. He read the text messages.

Greg: I got one. [Attachment: A photograph of Tom stand in the parking lot, unaware that he was having his picture taken]

Big Man: No shit?

Greg: Not shitting u. got this one at golf. So easy this one.

Big Man: He likes golf?

Greg: fuck if I kno. he was in the parking lot

Big Man: y tho?

Greg: beats me but hes perfect for us. Im at the restaurant. Bring Dillon

Big Man: haha that fucking guy? U sure??

Greg: Seriously bring him. I told him id let him in on the next one after he helped us with the Fort Lauderdale thing

Big Man: that was so fucked. What about Mr. Rogers??? That fucker cracks me up

Greg: no, just Dillon this time. R u at the office?

Big Man: nah I left for the day, Trish is handling the paperwork for that fucked up Garcia case I told u about

Greg: does trish like veal?

Big Man: stay away from my interns

Greg: w/e…Call Dillon and get over here

Big Man: k see you ina few

Company was on its way. Tom felt a little nervous about that. He knew the situation called for full-blown terror, but he was happy that something interesting was happening for a change.

Besides, in movies, the really scared characters always die the worst deaths. Tom hadn't lived long enough to be overly attached to life, but he definitely didn't want someone to cut him open and sew his chest cavity shut with beetles inside him or something.

His thoughts were interrupted by a knock on the back door and the sound of two men laughing at something one of them said.

Chapter 13

Arthur Tries to Pee on Mary

"You can be my toilet today, baby," Arthur declares, slapping the back of Mary's head a little too hard for it to be playful. "Are you ready for your bath?"

It's technically a shower, you drunk, Mary thinks. He is kneeling on a layer of black trash bags, still shivering from the AC.

"Daddy's going to *burp*... Daddy's going to piss the slut off your face and send you back to the dump," Arthur proclaims as he steps onto the glass coffee table, avoiding the abandoned plate and drinking glasses, and points his flaccid penis down at Mary.

Ah, that perfect jewel of improvisational verse was a golden shower in its own right, Mary thinks, impatiently waiting to get hosed with hot piss.

An uncomfortable moment passes. The sound of college basketball from the TV fills the silence.

"Hold on. I have a shy bladder."

Mary forgets that he's not supposed to talk and tries to console the man, "No worries, man, it happens to the best of us..." His voice comes out without a trace of effeminacy. Arthur looks down in a storm of homophobic rage.

"I TOLD YOLD YOU NOT —"

He slips on a puddle of condensation from the beer cans, spins, and falls into the glass table at an odd and painful-looking angle.

CRASH

Despite the dramatic fall, he tries to get up while finishing his sentence, shouting at the top of his lungs, "— TO TALK. YOU

FREAK, YOUR GAY-ASS VOICE MAKES THIS SHIT FEEL QUEER. YOU'RE SUPPOSED TO ACT LIKE A *REAL* SLUT AND NOT SAY SOME HOMO SHIT TO ME WHILE I'M TRYING TO PISS ON YOU! YOU MADE ME FUCK UP MY TABLE, YOU SHITBOX. LOOK AT THIS MESS! I'M GOING TO BREAK EVERY BONE IN YOUR FUCKIN…"

Arthur stops yelling. Confusion overcomes his feelings of rage. Something feels off. Arthur stares at Mary. Mary is standing a few feet away covered in a generous layer of air-drying breeder sauce with his jaw hanging open in disbelief.

Arthur slowly lifts a hand to his throat. A look of horror forms on his face. He tentatively touches the edge of a shard of glass lodged in his neck. All of the brutish intensity vanishes from his face. Mary looks up from Arthur's neck into the eyes of a scared child.

The crowd goes silent on the TV as a young man with a promising career ahead of him throws a basketball from halfway across the court, a split second before the buzzer sounds. The ball soars through the air in an elegant arc. Time dilates. No one breathes. The spinning orange ball passes through the hoop without touching the rim. Both teams jump off the bench as the crowd explodes in a rapture of shared ecstasy.

Arthur pulls the shard of glass out of his neck and looks at it. A spray of blood from his neck hits Mary in the cummy face. Arthur falls dead on the trash bags he had laid out for Mary.

Mary turns and watches the young basketball hero on the television as both teams lift him off his feet and carry him around the court, surrounded by a stadium of screaming fans. Everyone is jumping up and down as the hype sirens blast. The camera zooms in. The happiness radiating from the young man's face is almost blinding.

Chapter 14

Big Man and Dillon Enter the Restaurant

The knocking becomes more insistent. Tom could hear the two men wondering out loud why Greg hadn't opened the back door of the restaurant to let them in.

"Maybe he's taking a shit," said a man with the voice of a eunuch. The other guy didn't laugh.

"Nah, he wouldn't leave the brat unsupervised," said the second man. His voice sounded huge, even at a conversational volume. *That must be "Big Man,"* thought Tom.

He had hoped to just climb on a chair to unlock the back door and leave, maybe drive a car for the first time. Now that these goons were standing on the other side, that exit was no longer an option.

Tom used Greg's corpse as a bridge across the lake of blood and olive oil. The jukebox was now playing some song about a person named Mandy. The singer sounded totally in love with his own voice.

The knocking became a pounding.

If this were a movie, I'd be repeatedly dropping the keys while the bad guys start kicking down the door, thought Tom. He pulls the plug to the jukebox and crosses Greg bridge back into the kitchen to listen.

"What the fuck, Greg? Is this some kind of joke?"

"Just call his phone."

The phone in the kitchen started playing the same *"Do you think I'm Sexy?"* song from the car. Tom's heart skips a beat. *No. I don't think you're sexy, man.*

"He's not picking up."

"Text him."

The phone makes a boop.

Tom looked at Greg's bulky keyring. The front door had a whole colony of locks, and they all required keys. Who knows which key goes in which lock?

"Maybe he's hurt?"

"Shit, I didn't think of that."

"Should we kick in the door?"

Tom's eyes go wide.

"No, I don't want a shit show... This unit has roof access. Greg and I smoked a cigar up there, after that tasty little Boca girl he found at the mall."

"Why didn't you fuckers let me in on that one?"

"Because you're gross. Go get that ax from the trunk."

"Why do you need the ax?"

"The door up there has seen better days. It's locked from the inside, but it's just a panel of rotting wood on hinges."

"Why do you remember that... Were you casing this place? Did you scope out easy ways to break into my shit too?"

"You live in a trailer, Dill. So no, I haven't put a whole lot of thought into robbing you. Paying attention to detail is why I get more money for my clients than other attorneys."

"The first rung of that ladder is like eight feet off the ground. Maybe you can give me a boost, but I sure as shit can't pull your ass up after me. You're built like fucking Shaq, man."

"Are you really that simple? Greg's dumpster is on wheels. I'll just push that shit under it. Get the fucking ax. Dude could be bleeding out right now for all we know."

Tom felt cornered.

Every problem has a solution. His dad had said that during a long-winded speech about the necessity of divorce.

When life gives you crap, you find a toilet. He came up with that one himself.

Tom placed the keys gently on the counter next to Greg's phone. He hopped on Greg island to avoid the lava on his way to the hallway leading to the unisex restroom. Across from the bathroom, there was an unmarked door. He opened it.

Inside was a mop bucket, bottles of cleaning fluid, a stack of tattered looking towels, a couple of large boxes, a ladder to the square roof access door above. The rust-consumed lock hanging from the door looked like it was ready to crumble.

Tom looked inside one of the cardboard boxes: take-out containers. The other box was empty. He crawled inside the empty one and lowered the first box above him as he crouched, so it rested on the top of the one he was hiding in.

Just a couple of boxes in a storage closet – go on, see for yourself.

A few minutes passed. The box was getting hot inside, and Tom was sweating. He challenged himself to count backward from a thousand without forgetting what number he was on. He was in the mid eight hundreds when he heard the first ax blow make contact with the door above.

Eight hundred and sixty-two…

The ax fell a second time.

Eight hundred and sixty-one…

The third ax blow was followed by a loafer kicking in the rotted wood, a piece fell on the cardboard box above Tom and bounced off onto the floor loudly. Tom was shaking.

Eight hundred and sixty…

They climbed down the ladder.

"I don't hear him."

Eight hundred and fifty-nine…

A pant leg brushed Tom's cardboard sauna as the men left the cleaning supply room. He heard one of them wretch in the hallway.

"Guard that fucking door. This kid is not getting out of here!"

The door to the room Tom was in slammed shut.

He lost count.

"What the fuck happened to Greg?" Tom heard Dillon ask. The man was standing outside the door.

"The kid fucking stabbed him in the eye. This shit is a massacre. Looks like he's marinating him too."

"What?!"

Big Man didn't respond. He was too busy flipping over tables, trying to find whoever buried the knife in his best friend's leaky eye socket.

"Where is he?! What do you mean *marinating* him?!" shouted Dillon from the hallway, sounding frantic.

Big Man searched the kitchen, tearing the place apart. *Keep hiding, kid. I don't blame you. I'm going to deep-fry your head.*

"He poured olive oil on him or something! I don't fucking know, Dill, but the little fucker is definitely still in here!" Big Man screams from the kitchen as pots and pans crash around him violently. "Both the doors are locked, and Greg's keys are sitting right fucking here!"

Big Man tore open the stove and looked inside. Empty.

"FUCK!" he shouted as he punched a metal cabinet with a loud bang.

Chapter 15

The Pie is Too Hot

Mary feels a little emotional. He's still freezing. He finds the thermostat and turns it up to seventy-eight degrees.

The kid's big moment on TV made Mary feel weird. He feels happy for the guy, but witnessing all that triumph made him introspective. For a few minutes, everyone in that stadium loved and respected that kid. Mary is probably a couple of years older than him and hasn't achieved shit. He feels like his ship had sailed.

He gets to thinking about being loved. His sister might love him. She says she does. She took the time out of her day to give him a ride here. That was nice of her.

Mary thinks about a guy he sometimes fucks when he's desperate. The guy had said, "I love you" when he was blowing his load up Mary's ass recently. Mary had ghosted him for a month. He wonders now if the guy meant it.

Mary hikes up his skirt and sits on Arthur's toilet. He farts out the lube Arthur had jammed inside of him. *What does it all mean?*

He reaches for the toilet paper. There is none. *Shit.*

He squats in Arthur's bathtub and rinses himself with hot water from the faucet. He sniffs Arthur's shrunken bar soap. *That smells pretty nice.* His face feels like it's hosting a family reunion of bodily fluids. He wonders if peeling dried cum and blood off his cheeks would have an exfoliating effect. He opts for a good scrub instead.

He walks out of the bathroom with water dripping down his hairless body, not bothering to towel off. He looks around the bedroom.

One of those horrible printed canvases of the fancy-looking couple tango dancing on the beach is hanging on the wall. *Jeez.*

He looks through the dresser drawers. Arthur's wife must have packed most of her underwear. The one pair she left behind looks like a possum could take it skydiving.

He spots a picture frame next to a catchall dish shaped like a football. He picks it up and looks at it. *You're a big girl, aren't you?* The cursive tattoo beneath the woman's collar bone says *'Pennies from heaven…'*

Hmm.

Eh, I'd hit it, he thinks and sets the frame down where it was. He searches through Arthur's side of the dresser. Boxers. Socks. A handgun. *Oh, fun.*

Mary looks in the mirror above the dresser and poses with the handgun pointing at the mirror. The gun goes off, and the mirror explodes. The sound is apocalyptic. Mary's ears ring fiercely as he drops the weapon and staggers out of the bedroom.

WHAT THE FUCK, ARTHUR? Why wouldn't you have the safety switched on? That thing's trigger is fucking sensitive. He walks past the body on his way into the kitchen, patting at his ears, trying to stop the ringing.

He opens the fridge and removes a slice of blueberry pie that he noticed in his peripheral vision when he was fetching the six-pack for Arthur. He pulls back the plastic wrap and raises it to his nose. It doesn't smell old. He puts it in the microwave and nukes it for forty-five seconds.

The neighbor's dog hasn't stopped barking since the gun went off. *That dog is either really close or really loud. Man, I hope this ringing isn't permanent.*

The pie is steaming. Mary looks out the kitchen window while absent-mindedly blowing on a forkful of bubbling blueberry gunk. He shovels it into his mouth and screams. The dropped plate shatters. The roof of his mouth feels like it just got napalmed. He jams his head against the ice dispenser on the fridge. It makes grinding noises for what feels like eons and then finally dispenses its payload. He manages to catch one of the cubes in his mouth. He collapses next to the fridge, feeling traumatized. *Now that shit hurt.*

The dog is still going crazy out there. Mary wonders what kind of dog it is. The ringing in his ears slowly subsides.

Chapter 16

In a Box, under a Box

"I'm going to cut off your head, kid! It's only a matter of time…" Big Man thundered. A trashcan flew into a rack of hanging kitchen implements.

"Where the fuck is this kid?!" Dillon shouted nervously from the hallway.

"If I knew where he was, he'd be in a quiche by now! Check the fucking bathroom!" Big Man screamed across the restaurant.

"What if he's in there?!"

"Take the ax!"

Tom quietly lifted the box above him. He set it down next to the one he was standing in and stepped out onto the floor. He restacked the boxes and quietly stepped onto the first rung of the ladder. It creaked. He froze and listened to see if the men searching for him had heard.

"He's not in the bathroom!"

"Where the fuck is this kid?!"

He climbed to the roof and tiptoed to the exterior ladder at the edge. He could still faintly hear their frustrated shouting. He climbed down the ladder onto the dumpster and slid off its lid. There was now a second car parked a few spaces down from Greg's Buick.

Tom jogged over to it and peered into the window. There was a crossbow on the seat next to a box of manilla envelopes. A bag of produce had spilled onto the floormat. He tried the trunk, wondering if there would be any hacked-up bodies inside of it. It was open.

He expected to find a foot or something. He peered at the set of pricy looking golf clubs. He felt around in the pouch of the golf bag, removed a bright yellow golf ball, and he pocked it. He slid a putter out of the bag and shut the trunk. He walked around to the front of the strip mall, pretending the putter was a cane. The place was a ghost town.

Where am I? he wondered as he walked to the gas station at the corner of the parking lot. He went inside. The cashier, probably in his forties with skin the color of a paper bag, nodded at him politely. His thick eyebrows furrowed as they fell on the golf club.

"Can I help you, my small friend?" he asked Tom.

"Yeah, how far are we from Cherry Oak?"

"The apartment complex?" the man asked, again eyeing the putter with curiosity.

"My mom says we live in a townhome. She says it's better than an apartment because it has stairs."

"Ah, I see. Yes. Let me check." The man picks up his phone from the counter and looks up the community on his maps app. "This app says twelve minutes in a car, my friend."

"Thanks," Tom walks closer to the counter and asks, "Do you think this thing is worth any money?" He extends the club, inviting the man to inspect it.

The man looks at it carefully and nods, "That is a *very* nice putter. Are you a golfer, young man?"

"No, not really. Would you mind driving me home? I'm tired."

"I would be happy to, my friend, but I have a gas station to run."

Tom looks around. The man looks at Tom looking around and sees what he sees: not a customer in sight.

"How much do you think this club is worth?"

The man squints at it again to read the brand name. He searches on his phone browser. His eyebrows raise, "That is a four hundred dollar putter you have there."

"If my townhouse is twelve minutes from here, you could be back in twenty-four minutes."

"Yes, but what if someone wants to buy something?" The man gestures at the refrigerators and the racks of nearly expired snacks and adds, "I have a family to feed, you know."

"Do you like to golf?" Tom asks.

Chapter 17

Mary Meets Xena

The dog is still barking. Mary walks over to the neighbor's fence and squats down. The dog runs up to Mary barking. Mary offers the top of his hand for the dog to sniff. It sniffs Mary's knuckles through the chain-link fence and looks up at him. It looks it belongs in Alaska.

"Why are you in Florida?" Mary asks the husky.

Mary feels eyes on his back and turns to find their source: a woman in her thirties with short hair and crossed arms stands on the lawn behind him. She is scowling. *Hey, neighbor.*

"Doesn't this dog get hot under all this fur?" Mary asks the woman.

"She can come inside whenever she wants," the woman replies, looking at Mary's clothes without even trying to hide her disgust, "but she likes to keep an eye on things out here."

"What's her name?"

"Xena."

"Like the—"

"Yeah, like the TV show."

"Haha, I remember that show. Xena was one tough lady. She killed it with those bangs too, didn't she?"

"That's because she was a *real* woman," the neighbor remarks, eying Mary's pink pigtails.

Mary feels the sting of this comment. The woman still has her arms crossed like she's guarding her bosom. *What, is she afraid I'm going to run off with her tits?*

"Lucky lady. Some people would love to be a *real* woman," Mary responds with a note of melancholy, testing how unkind this woman is willing to be to a stranger.

The neighbor rolls her eyes and says, "I came out here because Xena was barking. She only barks at trouble," insinuating that Mary was trouble.

Ah yes, only such a perceptive animal would bark at a gunshot.

"I thought she was barking at that gunshot next door," Mary says.

"You heard that too?"

"Yeah, I'm pretty sure it came from inside that house," Mary says, pointing to Arthur's house, and then asks, "Do you think we should go over there and check if everyone is okay?"

"Arthur probably just got pissed at the game and shot his TV. I would not put it past him," she laughs. "He's straight as fuck, but he's a crazy motherfucker."

Oh, is he? And his name is Arthur, you say?

"He lives alone? What if he's hurt?"

"He doesn't live alone. His family is just out of town. Anyway, he's a big boy. He can take care of himself."

"You really think he just fired a gun in his own house? That sounds so dangerous."

"I don't fuckin' know. Might have even been a firework or some shit. Kids light fireworks around here all the time. Anyway, it's none of *my* business," the way she says this seems to imply that if it's none of *her* business, it's *definitely* none of Mary's.

"I guess it could have been one of the bigger ones, but I didn't see any fireworks…" he says as Xena prods the knuckle on his still extended hand with a wet nose.

"Don't put your hand so close to the fence. Xena doesn't like strange *boys* poking at her," she nods at the beware of dog sign. With this last barbed remark, she goes back inside the house. Mary gets a whiff of weed from the house before the woman closes her front door.

Damn, I want weed.

Xena looks at him with her tongue hanging out of her mouth. *Poor dog is burning up out here*, he thinks.

Mary goes back into Arthur's house. He retrieves a frozen sirloin from the freezer and walks past Arthur on his way back outside.

As he approaches the fence, Xena makes whinnying noises. She stands on her hind legs with her paws against the links, anxiously eyeing the contents of his hand with a look of wolfish blood lust. He reaches over the fence and hands her the frozen steak. She is so excited she leaps in place twice before backing into the meager shade of a decorative bush to lick at the refreshing meat popsicle.

Did you just wink at me, dog?

Chapter 18

Sheryl Confronts Tom

The man with the thick eyebrows from the gas station stopped his jeep at the entrance of Tom's development. Tom liked the man's music better than Greg's. No 'Rail Doorman,' or whatever that frisky dingus's name was. No 'Elvis' either. The girl singing in the Jeep sounded like she was straddling a jackhammer.

The man was all smiles the whole ride over but not creepy like Greg. He was just a hobbyist golfer with a beautiful new putter returning a precocious youngling to his nest.

Tom thanked him and hopped out of the Jeep. Before the man could drive away, Tom called out, "Wait!"

Tom had seen people taking cabs in many a movie. This Jeep wasn't a cab, but it felt like the same kind of transaction. He had used the club to pay for his fare, but he didn't have any money for the tip. He knew you were always supposed to tip your driver, and he didn't want to be rude. He reached into his pocket and walked around the Jeep to the driver-side window.

"Yes, my friend?" the man asked, looking down at the boy.

"Here's your tip," Tom handed him a bright yellow golf ball.

The man tried to keep a straight face while he thanked the boy and drove away laughing.

Tom went home and took a shower. He threw up a little – possibly from the whiskey, or maybe it was just stress. The drain was backed-up again. A triangle of partially digested sandwich meat floated across the soapy water. He hooked a finger down the drain and pulled up a clump of his mother's hair so thick and caked with drain scum that it looked like it was going to shake free and make a run for it.

He thought briefly about putting it in Aiden's house but tossed it in the toilet bowl next to the tub instead. As he watched the whirlpool form above the newly unclogged drain, he recalled all the little gifts he had snuck into Aiden's house.

1. An empty bottle of wine under the sink in the master bathroom
2. A shower cap stained with hair dye in the kitchen trash
3. The foil from a cigarette pack in a dish of candy by the magazines
4. Half of a flesh-colored crayon in the dryer
5. A half-empty tube of off-brand toothpaste in the shared bathroom medicine cabinet

After he had decided to sabotage their marriage and sue Sheryl for the inevitable inappropriate romantic advances she would make on him, his choice of items got more strategic:

6. A restaurant receipt in the pocket of a pair of dress slacks
7. A brochure for a hotel in Miami with a phone number written on it in bubbly handwriting tucked into a magazine about golf
8. A grubby tube of lipstick behind the toilet in the master bathroom
9. A hoop earing between the cushions of the sofa

He laughed one sharp laugh and then felt awkward for laughing by himself. He toweled off, walked into his bedroom, and there it was waiting for him: The silence of an empty home.

It was expanding. His ears felt funny. He took a deep breath and closed his eyes. His inhalation didn't feel like it had any oxygen in it. He felt dizzy. *I'm fine*, he said to himself. He went into the living room and turned on the TV. A teenage vampire was being told by a muscular friend that he had done something called "imprinting" on her baby. She seemed pretty upset about it.

He turned off the TV. The silence returned. He went into the kitchen and turned on the garbage disposal and the sink. He got on a chair and fed an empty paper towel roll into the ravenous drain.

It wasn't working. He couldn't keep the garbage disposal running indefinitely. Silence waited for him beneath the racket. He turned off the garbage disposal and ran into his room, screaming rap lyrics. He put on clothes in a rush and jogged over to Aiden's.

Aiden's mom answered the door. She looked like she wanted to drill holes in his vital organs. She had never looked at him like this before.

"We need to have a chat, you little sociopath," she said in the hushed whisper-growl that comes out of moms that are dangerously close to breaking character. She grabbed him by the back of his shirt and led him into her bedroom.

"Where's Aiden?" he asked her while being dragged, trying to feel out the lay of the land.

"Aiden is at a friend's house. A *real* friend," she snarled at him. He wondered what real friends Aiden had? He seemed like such a lump. He was spoiled, but he didn't share his stuff, so he wasn't exactly a beacon of irresistible friendship.

"Where the ffu… HELL did you get this?!" she was shaking a small purply looking object in his face, "and WHY did you put it in our bedroom?!" She had a vice grip on his shoulder and a crazy mom look on her face.

His heart felt like horse hooves. He was busted. *Or was he?*

He squinted at the thing in her hand. It was a human toe – a man's toe but with a painted toenail. *That's a gorgeous blue*, he caught himself admiring the polish and then shook free from her grasp and took two purposeful steps back.

"Why do you have that?!" he demanded indignantly. He was confused and a little fearful about this unexpected development.

"Because a little demon child pretending to be a sweet boy has been leaving shi… GARBAGE in my house!" she was glaring into his face while she hissed. After an awkward moment, her face softened slightly. She had expected guilt or defensiveness, but the kid just looked bewildered. She could tell by his facial expression that she had gravely miscalculated, "You didn't… you didn't leave this in my house?"

For a moment, she looked relieved. The idea that such a polite boy, such a good listener, would be sneaking human body parts into her house when she wasn't looking had disturbed her. The relief was temporary.

"But if it wasn't you, then…" her eyes widened in a look of growing fear as she realized the implications of Tom's innocence.

"Its toenail kind of looks like a windshield," Tom offered awkwardly. Aiden's mom fetched him a soda and a fistful of hard candy and sent him on his way.

Chapter 19

Some Texts from the Wife

Xena looks up from her frozen steak. Her creepy husky eyes shine with adoration for Mary.

Mary glances around the neighborhood. The houses come in a few different models, but the paint colors and landscaping are all similar. Mary wonders what inspired the HOA to limit residents to three neutered shades of taupe. The color looked like the matte frosting on the kind of donut no one ever ordered.

I guess these days people hear a gunshot and just shrug? None of my business, they're all probably thinking. This isn't even a financially challenged neighborhood. These people are just too busy binge-watching crime shows to be bothered by gunshots, I guess.

Visible heat rises off the street in waves. There are vehicles in front of some of the homes, but there isn't another soul in sight. Xena and Mary have the place to themselves. Mary walks along Xena's chain-link fence to get a look at the neighbor's backyard.

No kiddy pool. No swing set. No barbecue. No garden. Just a thirsty looking tree and an outdoor carpet of regulation suburban grass. *This is no breeder house*, Mary observes. The curtains are drawn. The shades are shut. Unlike Arthur's house, this woman's master bathroom has an exterior door leading onto the patio. The patio is just a slab of unwashed pavement harboring a plastic outdoor table with an ashtray packed with soggy cigarette butts. The door to the bathroom is fitted with a doggy door big enough for a *real* woman.

Mary walks back around the house, waving at Xena, and then feeling awkward about it. Xena looks up from the steak thawing between her paws. She gazes at him lovingly as he passes.

Back in the house, he searches for Arthur's phone and finds it – in addition to his keys and wallet – in the pocket of a pair of shapeless blue jeans in a pile by the bed. He reads the name on the driver's license, 'Arthur Reed.'

He checks the phone. There is a new text message from Mrs. Reed.

Mary scrolls back to read their conversation starting from yesterday morning:

Arthur: It's only a week babe

Babe: Presha misses you

Arthur: I miss Presha's mommy

Presha? Holy shit, I wonder who dreamed up that little moniker. Girl's going to grow up to be a diet-vitamin reseller.

Babe: Did you get around to doing those hedges?

Arthur: It's fucking hot down here babe

Babe: That girl Megan next door just pays guats to do it

Arthur: thats too expensive

Babe: So is getting fined by the hedge nazis

Arthur: I said ill do it

Babe: I miss my curly bear

Yikes.

She sent the 'curly bear' text when Mary was outside scrutinizing their neighbor's backyard. *Megan, huh? Megan must be Xena's mommy. Megan is kind of mean.*

Mary sends Arthur's wife a text, *miss you too babe*. He doesn't want her to spend her vacation worrying about her curly bear. After a moment, he decides to add, *I did the hedges.*

Mary pulls down his skirt and squeezes out of the damp sequined tube top. He pulls back the straps on his pink Velcro sneakers and pulls off his ruffle socks. He walks around the house naked, with his pink pigtails bobbing, shutting the blinds on all the windows and pulling the curtains closed over the sliding glass doors.

He collapses on the leather sofa and falls asleep, flipping through the channels.

Chapter 20

Young Tom Paints His Nails

Tom finishes his juice box. He throws away the old people candy. *Butterscotch? Really?*

He was still pretty confused about the whole ordeal he had just been privy to. He didn't put that toe there. *Why was there a toe in her house? What was such pretty nail polish doing on a man's toe?*

This thought led him to think about nail polish. His mom had nail polish.

He turned on the TV. A movie about the mafia was playing. Some guy's body was bouncing on the floor as three men unloaded their machine guns on him.

He painted his nails. He liked the bright colors. He had gotten some of the polish on the skin framing the nail, but he examined his handiwork with a sense of pride nonetheless. He thought his hands looked pretty.

On TV, a man was lowered into the ocean screaming, his feet encased in a block of concrete. He was begging his captors with real emotion. Tom felt bad for the guy. *Drowning must suck.*

He nodded off, sitting there by himself in the living room. He dreamed that his hair was growing rapidly. He kept trying to cut it with scissors, but no matter how hard he tried, more just pushed out from his bleeding scalp. Faceless dream people with machine guns kept stepping on it and saying, "Oopsie! Sorry, young man."

He looked up at the throbbing dream sun. It was a beautiful shade of blue.

Chapter 21

Introducing Kim

Kim slides off the poll and crawls across the strobing plexi platform. *Ah, a fish out of water,* she thinks as she leans over the rail towards a terrified looking guy in a Hawaiian shirt. She pulls his head between two beautiful manufactured breasts and shakes from side to side. Her skin is so white the boy can see the lines of her veins spread across the contours of her abdomen like the blueprints of a house he can't afford.

He nervously tucks singles into her G-string as she breathes the words *thank you* into his fleshy little ear.

She leans back on one hand and dances suggestively with her pelvis. The prey gives her thigh a tentative squeeze, gaining courage from the choreography of her perfectly rehearsed bodily sales pitch.

She pulls aside her G-string with her short black fingernails, exposing herself to him. She sinks back onto her elbows, elevating her hips, then lowers her butt onto the flashing platform and spreads her legs, scooting closer to the side rail. She hooks her heels around the metal blacking of the boy's chair. She raises her vagina towards his hypnotized face. She presses the soft hood of her clit against the tip of his nose. *Boop.*

The runt busts in pants. Kim frees him from the cage of her legs. He sets a pile of crumpled ones on the platform. She raises a predatorial eyebrow. He looks away, sheepishly, and dispenses the rest of her withdrawal. She rewards him with a conspiratorial wink as she crawls to the next human ATM. The warm cum soaking into his briefs turns cold against his thigh in the frigid air of the club. He gets up and limps away.

"So soon?" the girl in fishnets at the door teases him playfully. He doesn't respond as he pushes open the massive doors on his way to the parking lot.

"We hope to see you again soon, Sir," the bouncer says in a consoling tone. Every night, he watches guys like this come in all nervous and excited. Every night, he watches them shuffle out into the parking lot, broke and embarrassed. He watches the poor sap skulk past the decorative stone gargoyle on his way to his car. *Drive safe, brother.*

Inside, Kim's second song finishes. Dave comes out from behind the curtain and brooms up the cash. Kim carefully descends the stairs off the platform after sliding back into the negligee she discarded at the beginning.

She walks behind the velvet curtain and pours water into a paper cup at the cooler. She is draining a second cup when Dave passes through the curtain with the money pouch. She likes Dave. He's the kind of guy that moves through life in a bubble of peace – a rare quality in a man.

She thinks about the first night she danced here at The B&B. A door girl had ushered her into the office upstairs for an interview and left her there to wait for the owner to get back from dinner. Dave was sitting on a black sofa against the opposite wall, resting his eyes. She remembers being so nervous when she entered the room. She looked over at him, sitting there with his eyes closed, and just felt calmer for some reason.

After twenty minutes, he got up to leave. He shared his mantra as he passed her on his way to the door. "Nothing to worry about," he had said. And there hadn't been. The owner had come in a few minutes later, apologizing for being so late. He gave her a quick speech about the pay structure and the house rules before shaking her hand and telling her to go have fun.

"How did we do?" she asks Dave. The sweeper doesn't count the bills until it's time to go home, but Dave has been a money guy for so long, he can just tell.

"Looked like a little under a grand. You go up again after Amber and Shell. Nice to see so many guests at the stage."

She smiles and tosses her paper cup into the wastebasket. She goes back into the dressing room to change into her next outfit.

In the back of the club, at a private table, Big Man Jr. slides an olive off the plastic sword from a now-empty martini. His joyless eyes stare into the past as he chews. Today was the fifth anniversary of his father's violent death. Memories of the security camera footage distract him from the dancers. He recalls his father's look of panic as his skull was bludgeoned with a hammer. He recalls the pixelated face of his father's killer.

Chapter 22

An Innocent Boy Dies, and No One Cares

Dillon and Big Man left Greg's corpse in the restaurant to search for the kid. *What if he rats?* The gas light illuminates moments after they pull out of the parking space. *MOTHER FUCKER, WHY NOW?*

They pulled into the gas station by the restaurant. Dillon left Big Man at the pump to run inside and buy a carton of cigarettes, but the door was locked. There was a handwritten sign taped to the door:

"Back in 24 minutes."

"Shit," Dillon said to himself as he jogged back to the Lincoln. Big Man looks back at Dillon as he replaces the pump and screws on the gas cap. "Fucker's on break," Dillon informed him.

"That lazy fuck," Big Man replied, scoping out the surrounding area for movement. They got back into the car and peeled out. Five minutes later, a Jeep pulled into the parking lot. The driver hopped out and walked to the door, twirling a putter and whistling.

Big Man and Dillon drove around the surrounding neighborhood, scanning for the boy that had somehow escaped the restaurant. Dillon retrieved the crossbow from the backseat and set it on his lap.

"Little shit's on foot. He couldn't have gotten far."

"What if he got picked up by someone else?"

"I hope he fucking did. I hope some cheesy motherfucker has the kid simmering in a big blue barrel. I just don't want him out here yammering about the restaurant to some good fucking samaritan. The last thing we need is a bunch of pigs sniffing around that place.

Even if Greg's body wasn't swimming around the bar, there's plenty of..."

"I meant if he hitchhiked, you spooky little imp. Some uppity cunt sees a kid trying to hitchhike, she'd get nosy real fast. This is a fucking mess. This is worse than Greg's drag queen shit in Fort Lauderdale."

"Ahh, the teacher! He tasted like hummus," Dillon recalled fondly.

"What the fuck are you talking about? We didn't even eat that motherfucker."

"I was talking about his peepee."

"I worry about you sometimes, Dillon."

"Hey, worry about me all you like, I fucking cleaned that shit up tidy for you guys – the queeny teacher and the kid both. Fuckers are still posting flyers looking for those two. They saw those photos I found of the queer wearing a dress, and that's all they needed to see," Dillon bragged. "Those dumb fuckers are convinced the teacher took him to Mexico or some shit. Yeah, I cleaned my fucking plate on that one."

"That's why Greg had me call you on this one. It was his way of thanking you."

"Aw, Greg. I'm going to miss that—"

Big Man snapped his fingers, interrupting Dillon's lament. He pointed across the empty lot. A young boy was walking alone on the side of a drainage ditch. Big Man pulled his phone out of his pocket and pulled up the text with Greg. He enlarged the photo and scrutinized it.

Greg's phone had a shit camera, and he had taken the picture through his car window, but the kid's clothes matched. In the photo, Tom is wearing a plain white t-shirt and blue jeans. It was blurry, but Big Man thought he had the same hair cut too. He turned the Lincoln at the corner of the dirt lot and accelerated.

"LET'S GET HIM!" shouted Dillon excitedly as they sped towards the boy. After a cursory look around to check for possible witnesses, Dillon rolled down his window and aimed the crossbow. The kid heard an approaching vehicle. He turned to look. A bolt slid out the flight groove of the crossbow like a bobsled and lodged itself in the boy's brain. He fell in a heap. In less than 30 seconds, he was in the trunk next to the golf clubs with his leaking head wrapped tightly in a trash bag.

Big Man pulled away, closing Greg's text to open his streaming music app. His giant thumb came down on the play button like a judge's gavel. A single snare strike bit the speakers, and then there was Judas Priest:

BREAKIN' THE LAW! BREAKIN' THE LAW!

Chapter 23

The Night That Changed Kim's Life

Kim leaves The B&B Gentlemen's Club at 2:15 am, accompanied by one of the club's guests. In four years of stripping, she has never left the club with a customer – never even gave out her phone number. She views the club's clientele as anthropomorphic checking accounts. In other words, she doesn't take their marriage proposals to heart.

"How are you tonight, Misty?" the bouncer asks, addressing Kim by her stage name. He sees dancers leave with guys every night but never Kim. She usually exits out of the staff door wearing plain clothes and sneakers. He's surprised to see her hobbling out the front door, still on prop-heels, pulling one of the guests by his hand like she's taking him to the back room (instead of dragging him into the parking lot).

He isn't being nosy. He just wants to make sure she hasn't been drugged or something. He tries not to catch feelings too hard, but he cares about these girls.

"I'm great, Carlos. How's your night going?" Kim responds with enough clarity to relieve him of his concerns.

"A little buggy, but I can't complain. Be safe out there tonight," he says and gives the man she is with a long look, memorizing his features, *just in case*.

The club's house rules prohibit dancers from leaving with guests, but the rules are strictly a legal precaution. Most of the girls don't even have them memorized. The strip clubs in South Florida don't use yardsticks to separate their patrons from the talent. The whole state is shaped like a penis. In a penis-shaped state, handjobs are handshakes.

Like the rest of the dancers, Kim breaks the house rules nightly. She could make decent money just dancing, but she feels like an idiot turning down some of these guys' desperate offers. They are willing to pay out the nose for things she used to do for free.

One time, a drunk daytrader offered her three thousand dollars to put his balls in her mouth during a private dance. She used the money to go to Jamaica. Those fifteen inconsequential seconds bankrolled her entire trip. She spent a weekend smoking weed all day and happily stuffing jerk chicken into the same mouth the guy had dunked his balls in. *Who the fuck cares?*

She would tug a guy's cock in the booth a couple of times and then start acting bored until he pulled out his wallet. She paid off the remainder of what she owed on her hatchback a week after she started dancing. She paid off all her credit cards in the first six months. When a lonely boy blows his paycheck in her mouth, she knows what she is really swallowing: the past two weeks of his life. She hasn't forgotten where she came from.

Before she started batting bills out of boys with her boobs, she was working double shifts putting oily food that smelled like shit in front of oily families that tipped like shit.

Her one big mistake? She paid her rent on a credit card one fucking time, and the interest accumulated faster than her paychecks. She had to apply for two more cards and use cash advances to pay the minimums on the first card. By the time she was twenty-seven, she was living in an efficiency apartment by herself, saddled with twelve thousand dollars of credit card debt and nothing to show for it.

She remembers every detail of the night that changed her life. She was working late, and one of her tables was a young guy eating by himself. He had looked at her with bloodshot eyes and ordered chicken fingers, a bacon cheeseburger, an order of broccoli, and "vodka… lots of vodka." He had a small cartoon thumbs-up tattooed an inch from his right eye. The smell of weed coming off him was so potent she felt like he had a pound of it stashed under his beanie.

She had missed weed so bad back then. Everyone she knew that could get her weed had gradually drifted out of her orbit. People got married. Breeders had kids. To her, this guy smelled like good times.

When he finished his dinner, she asked him if he wanted anything for dessert. He drained his fourth shot and smiled. His smile was so innocent and genuine that his response caught her off guard, "Honestly…" he appeared to be putting effort into focusing his eyes for long enough to read her nametag, "Honestly Kim, the only thing I want for dessert is my waitress' vagina… maybe with a hot squirt of bodily fluids."

At first, she put her hands on her hips and said, "*Excuse* me?" but he was still looking at her like he hadn't just said something weird and vulgar. "Please, don't be gross, dude. I'm just trying to do my fucking job here and go home. I meant ice cream or something."

"*Kimmmmm*, there is nothing 'gross' about a handsome young man snacking on his exhausted waitress in a mutually consenting atmosphere. *You* asked if I wanted dessert. If your pussy isn't on the menu, I will settle for your fartbox." He lost it when he said the word 'fartbox.' His laughter was weirdly contagious. She suppressed the urge to laugh and tried to stay angry.

"You don't even look old enough to drink, kid. I fucking gave you drinks cause you looked sad. I can't even *believe* what I'm fucking hearing right now. The shit I put up with. You know, you really shouldn't fuck with the people that serve you food," she said, trying to sound threatening.

"Kim, if making a straightforward request to clean you like a momma cat is 'fucking with you,' then I'm sorry," he paused for a moment to smile lovingly at her. "Curiosity is killing me now. If a person were to 'fuck with' their waitress, would she piss in his... I mean, *their* drink?" He moved his eyebrows up and down suggestively. "You know... like out of revenge or whatever? It would be uh, *hate* pee."

She was unable to respond. She didn't know whether to break his nose on the table or give in to great gushes of long-suppressed laughter at the sheer gall of this guy.

She would protect her honor, she decided. She would tell this kid off. She would slap him in his not unattractive face. Her voice returned.

"FIRST OF ALL..." she began her glorious and empowering verbal takedown but then stopped short. He was holding his fork and knife like a hungry cartoon wolf and staring at her crotch.

"Kim, is everything alright over there?" asked the elbow-touchy-would-be-night-in-shining-armor bartender from behind the bar. She had seen him throw out guys for coming onto the younger female barbacks. He would put on a pageant of chivalrous valor and then hit on those same girls himself.

"We don't even have to have sex, Kim. You can just piss in my mouth. I want to swallow something that's been in your body," said the potty-mouthed young stoner at the table. "I have so much weed, Kim. SOO much."

"Yeah, everything's fine over here. I know this guy," she responded to the would-be heroic bartender. He rolled his eyes and turned around to offer a pregnant woman another round.

Kim leaned over and whispered in the guy's ear, "Fuck it, I'll piss in your mouth. My shift ends in an hour."

"Kim, you are a perfect tangerine. I'll take the check now, please."

Chapter 24

Dead Arthur Buys Mary a Thing

Mary wakes up on Arthur's leather sofa. It's 7:34 pm. He's naked. His neck is sore. *Truly, this is a bad couch.*

Arthur smells.

Mary leans forward and takes an unopened beer from the bloody wreckage of the coffee table. There's an infomercial about an abnormally powerful blender on the TV.

He absentmindedly cracks open the can and takes a long sip of its lukewarm contents as he watches the program with interest.

"And this baby will blend ANYTHING," says an almost giddy looking bearded man in an apron.

"Not *anything*?" the blonde co-host says with theatrical skepticism.

"ANYTHING!" the host shouts as he pounds his fist on the counter. He cackles like a homeless scientist and turns his attention to the woman beside him.

"What about…" she pauses for drama, "…this broomstick?" She pulls a broom from behind the set's counter.

Mary leans forward. *There is no fucking way they are going to be able to blend that broomstick!*

The man looks towards the crowd like they are all secretly aware of how dumb his co-host's question is. He pumps his fist three times in the air and points to them as they all scream, "ANYTHING!!"

They blend the broomstick.

No. Fucking. Way.

They blend a toy car.

Metal?! You've got to be kidding me!

They blend a screwdriver.

A SCREWDRIVER???

They blend a cup of marbles.

I NEED THIS. I NEED TO OWN THIS.

They blend a box of contractor screws.

WHY HASN'T THE GOVERNMENT STOPPED THESE PEOPLE? IT'S TOO MUCH POWER!

Everything that enters the death-giving maw of this insane blender comes out as powder so fine that it's a breathing hazard.

Mary looks over at the discarded silicone dildo. He looks at the remote control. He looks at the empty beer cans. He looks at Arthur's rigid body, lying on a bed of trash bags. He imagines feeding a fork into the blender and seeing it reduced to silt.

Mary grabs Arthur's cellphone and searchers for the blender on Amazon. The ratings are outstanding. Reviewers share photographs of their bizarre blending adventures.

He looks at the price. It's $599. *Jeez,* Mary recoils at the price.

Mary lives off small lump sums like a chicken fetus lives off an embryonic sac. He doesn't have expendable income. In exchange for this monetary disability, he is free from a degrading nine-to-five job. He has often imagined what working would be like: Talking people into changing their cable packages. Refolding shirts customers drop on the floor in some sweatshop-sponsoring retail hell. *No thanks.*

Necessity forces most people into bondage, but Mary doesn't live in bondage (well, not in that sense of the word anyway). Having grown up watching his mom work her life away, he never developed a taste for trading his soul for puka shells. When she died unceremoniously in a late-night car accident coming home from work, he made up his mind: *Fuck that shit.*

After his dad remarried, living with an adult daughter had started to feel like a buzzkill. Buying a little house for his kids fed two birds with one seed; it got Gwen out of the nest, and it assuaged his parental guilt about neglecting his maladjusted son. When Gwen finished school and got stable work, their dad and his new wife moved to New Jersey.

Mary looks up from Arthur's phone at the television. The host is flashing a maniacal grin as he dangles his car keys above the blender. *I want to blend car keys*, sulks Mary.

He picks up Arthur's wallet. He uses one of Arthur's cards and the information on his driver's license to open a dummy prime account and adds the blender to his online shopping cart. He almost makes the purchase but hesitates.

He adds the following items to his shopping cart:

- fishnet bodystocking
- rhinestone-studded faux leather choker
- novelty sunglasses
- shiny purple underwear
- bright orange nail polish
- dish soap (Gwen said they were out)
- watch with a poodle on the dial
- pair of flipflops
- six months worth of meal replacement powder

- shaving razors (for Gwen)
- numerous hair products

He adds a multivitamin at the last minute… *you never know, they might do something*. The cart total is pretty severe. He decides to split the order on multiple cards from Arthur's wallet. He selects next day shipping for everything and places the order.

He peels his butt cheeks off the leather sofa. The seam of the cushion is imprinted across the back of his thigh. He rubs his right cheek tenderly to encourage circulation. Arthur's phone buzzes. He has received a new text message.

Chapter 25

Kim, Unchained

The night Kim had brought the stoner guy his check (after agreeing to piss in his mouth), she had unknowingly taken her first step into a whole new life.

She hadn't agreed exclusively because of his weed comment. Yeah, she wanted to smoke, but it was more than that. She had been groping along an invisible wall, searching for the door out of her shitty life; his vulgar invitation had been the hidden doorknob.

She was tired of being Kim, the waitress who gets shit tipped because a salad didn't have enough croutons. She was tired of being Kim, the wage-slave who works an exhausting job only to go home deeper in debt. Making the right decisions had created this shitty life that she hated living. That night in the restaurant, she had tried making the wrong decision for a change.

She remembers feeling a little disappointed when she came to pick up the check, and he was gone. That changed quickly. The cover of the waiter's wallet she had dropped the receipt off in was open at a 45-degree angle. She opened it and gasped at the wad of cash it contained. She placed her hand on the table for support.

She looked around quickly to see if anyone was paying attention. She tucked the cash into her apron. Beneath the money, a note was written on the receipt next to a poorly drawn winky face:

Good luck, Kim

She was excited, confused, and nervous. She tried her best to act casual as she walked to the register. She paid the kid's bill with one of the many hundreds he had left her, sliding the change into her apron with the rest of the cash.

"You've got some shady friends," the rapey bartender said as she passed the bar on her way to the bathroom.

"I need to take my break," she responded.

"I don't blame you. That guy was on drugs," he called after her as she entered the ladies' room.

The bathroom was empty. Kim let herself exhale the breath she had been holding in. In the mirror, her reflection was smiling at her. It *never* did that.

She went in the handicap stall and pulled the money out of her apron. She counted it – ten thousand dollars minus what she had used to pay the guy's check. *What the fuck?*

After her shift that night, she waited on the bench outside for fifteen minutes. She was nervous about walking home at night with all that money, and it was only getting later. Her apartment complex was a fifteen-minute walk from her job.

When she was satisfied that he wasn't coming back, she started for home. She clutched her purse tightly against her body and walked quickly, looking around for threatening characters but trying not to be too obvious about it.

She walked past a homeless woman sleeping on a bus bench. The lady reeked. She turned around, hating herself for what she was about to do. She carefully tucked two of the hundreds into the homeless woman's jacket and quickly walked away.

Ugh, I'm so fucking stupid. What if someone saw and suspects that I'm carrying a bunch of cash?

She came to an intersection and pressed the walk button. It was a stiflingly humid night, and she was perspiring. There was a tall man with dark skin smiling at her from across the street. He had a backpack over his shoulder, and he was holding something in a brown bag. The signal changed to walk.

"Hey, little lady," the man said to her as she approached.

"Hey, Louis. How are you?" she asked. He worked at the grocery store lottery counter. He always teased her for her monthly five-dollar scratch-off purchases, telling her she might as well be burning the money.

"I'm better now that my shift is over," he said as he took a sip of the orange juice bottle in the paper beverage bag that he was holding. "How about you?"

"I'm pretty great, actually," she responded cheerfully.

"It's nice to see you in a good mood for a change," he said kindly.

"Trust me, it's nice to be in one," she responded.

She told him to have a nice weekend, and he told her to do the same. She continued walking home.

She was almost there when the white unmarked van pulled up beside her on the street. She paused and looked at the van. The passenger side window rolled down slowly. The man in the van was wearing a mask over his mouth. He waved for her to come closer.

"Sorry about the mask. I have a cold, and I'm trying not to get my aunt sick," he said, gesturing at the seat next to him with his thumb. The driver, a friendly-faced older woman with red curly hair, leaned over and waved at Kim. She waved back.

The masked man asked, "Do you know where there's an animal hospital around here? My phone is dead, and my aunt refuses to carry one. We accidentally clipped a turtle that was crossing the street, and he's in pretty bad shape."

"Oh my God, that's horrible," she said. "There is one on Forrest Hill just west of the I95 off-ramp. You can't miss it."

They thanked her as they pulled away. Kim kept walking, feeling the cash through the fabric of her purse. She could see the apartments in the distance.

Just as she entered the seemingly deserted parking lot of her apartment complex, a group of teenage boys emerged from the bushes and rushed towards her.

"Hi," one of the boys awkwardly murmured as they passed her on their way to the vending machine by the community mailbox.

"Give me the money!" she heard one of the boys say to his friend as they surveyed the packaged contents of the machine. She climbed the steps to the second floor and walked down the poorly lit hallway to her apartment.

He was standing in front of her door by a puddle of dirty water left from that afternoon's thunderstorm. He stared at her with dark emotionless eyes. He licked his lips.

Chapter 26

Meat, Blood, and Bleach

Big Man pulled the Lincoln behind Greg's Buick. Dillion hopped out with Greg's keys and re-parked the dead man's car, so the Lincoln had enough space to park closer to the restaurant's back door. Dillon walked quickly to the door and opened it. Big Man hopped out and took a quick survey of their surroundings. They were alone.

He popped the trunk. They carried the body of the boy they thought was Tom into the kitchen. Dillon ran back out to shut the trunk of the Lincoln and parked it behind one of the neighboring units. He rejoined Big Man in the kitchen and locked the door behind them.

Big Man had already started cutting into the boy's body with the practiced hands of a chef. Ordinarily, they would have taken turns playing with their food first, but they were both tired, and the boy was already getting cold.

Big Man found sustenance in harming the innocent. He felt nourished by the fear of children. He also knew some exquisite preparations of long pig. Greg's primary enjoyment had always come from the hunt. That doesn't mean he didn't enjoy resting in the shade of a young tree. Dillon was just a pedophile.

"Little fucker," Big Man addressed the rack of ribs he was prepping. "I still don't know how the fuck you did it, kid."

"What if he went out the roof exit?" Dillon said thoughtfully as he filled the mop bucket with a mixture of bleach and water from the tap.

"That shit was locked from inside, Dill." The tone of Big Man's voice betrayed the discomfort he felt, not knowing the answer to this puzzle.

"Well, regardless, we got fuckin' lucky, Big. That could have been bad," Dillon said to draw Big Man out of his reverie.

After the boy's body had been prepped, parceled, and neatly wrapped in butcher paper, Big Man started on the less enjoyable task of breaking down Greg. Dillon made a supply run before the hardware store closed. He repaired the roof door and cleaned up the place while he waited for Big Man to finish, and then he mopped the whole restaurant.

The air was sharp with bleach. While Dillon mopped up Greg's blood, Big Man searched through Greg's books to mop up the dead man's life. He located the contact information of the restaurant's three employees and texted them from Greg's phone, thanking them for their service, but informing them that he could no longer afford to keep the restaurant.

Greg had paid his staff their pitiful wages nightly in cash for a variety of unscrupulous reasons. Gigi, who waited tables, texted back a simple and eloquent *fuck you*. Big Man turned off Greg's phone.

Greg had often lied about having kids and a big house to make the children he kidnapped feel safe with him, but in reality, he lived alone in a shithole weekly rental. The restaurant enabled him to get creative with his taxes, but his real income came from trading SD cards (full of the kind of images you can't unsee) to jaded perverts for envelopes of cash.

It was almost sunrise by the time Big Man slid the Buick key from Greg's keyring and handed it to Dillon. It had been an exhausting night, but at least he got a nice car out of it. Dillon drove back to the trailer park with mixed emotions; he had lost a friend, but his new ride was fucking sweet.

Big Man had one stop to make before he drove home to his sleeping wife. Lidia would probably baby him for working so hard to support her and Big Man Jr. She associated his absences with her ever-increasing credit card limits.

Greg's place was surprisingly clean, given the location. Big Man put Greg's laptop and film equipment in a trash bag. He lifted the mattress and sighed. Over six hundred thousand dollars of neatly banded cash stacks lined the boxspring. He was going to miss Greg. The guy was one hell of a businessman.

Big Man packed up the cash and threw the electronics bag in his trunk. He spent the drive home turning the situation over in his head, trying to figure out what the hell happened that afternoon. He never did figure it out.

Back at the restaurant, Greg's remnants fizzed in a barrel of acid placed under the extractor hood of the kitchen's ventilation system. The boy's meat waited quietly in the freezer while less than a mile away, his one living parent snorted coke-flavored baby laxatives off of a urinal.

Over the next week, Big Man's oblivious family lavishly praised the many dishes the boy became, but they absolutely raved about his preparation of coriander and cumin roasted rack of pork with five-spice puree. He served it with a clever chile, pumpkin seed, and cilantro salad.

After they finished, Lidia demanded to know why her pork never tasted that good. He told her it had been a special locally-butchered Houdini suckling.

Chapter 27

Arthur's ~~Bitchy~~ Horny Neighbor

Mary turns off the TV and reads the new text message on Arthur's phone. He raises his eyebrows in surprise.

Megan: Hi

Mary is curious why the bitchy lady with the overheating wolf in her yard is texting her neighbor's husband. His curiosity eats at his guts until he gives in and texts her back.

Arthur: sup??

Megan: Touchin my pussy cause ur too busy to do it for me

Mary runs around the house naked, jumping up and down, giddy with nervous energy. HOLY SHIT, ARTHUR WAS FUCKING THE NEIGHBOR!

Arthur: wish I could but im not even home right now

Megan: some fag in a skirt said it heard a gunshot come from ur house. Mb u shud come home and check on it lol

Arthur: prbly just pranking you. ive seen him hangin around the park… fucking queer

Megan: Cancer

Arthur: I kno. fuck him. Send me pics

Megan: u have to delete

Arthur: I always delete shit. Presha plays games on my phone

Mary smiles. He still can't get over the fact Arthur and his wife named their kid "Presha."

Megan: fcuk me [Attachment: A hazy photograph of a woman's vagina spread open by two fingers]

Arthur: mmm

Megan: put it in here too [Attachment: The face of the woman Mary had spoken to outside with a finger pointing to her open mouth, tongue extended]

Mary does another lap around the inside of the house. He can't stop laughing at his good fortune. When he manages to collect himself, he picks up the phone and responds.

Arthur: wish I were there

Megan: sent me ur dik

Arthur: cant right now sorry

Megan: NOT FAIR

Mary looks over at Arthur's corpse. The man died trying to pee on his face. His penis had stiffened when he bled out, but it's the wrong color now. Mary takes a couple of shots of Arthur's death erection, experimenting with multiple angles. He shakes the phone a little to cause blur.

Megan: SHOW ME UR FUCKIN COCK I SENT U MY PUSSY BICH

She's getting impatient. Mary sends her a text to buy some time.

Arthur: Mmm you make me hard

Megan: SHOW MEEE

Mary downloads a photo editing app and shifts the hue on one of the photos. He settles for an angle looking up at the shaft with a background of bush and blurry stomach.

Megan: FUCK U

Mary increases the saturation and texts the photo to Megan. He waits anxiously. A couple of minutes pass.

Megan: mmm I want that in me

Megan: come home and smoke w me

Mary wishes Megan was talking to him and the dead guy stinking up the living room. Arthur died before Mary could get off. He's still horny. Megan's vagina had the mystique of being forbidden, and her mouth may be a source of barely literate hate slurs, but it's attached to the head of a person that has weed.

Mary's inner demons begin whispering with voices like sweet tinkling bells. A plan is forming in his mind. Before he even fully comprehends its intricacies, he knows he will follow through. His priorities are clear to him. The path beckons.

Arthur: you want to come over when I get home?

Megan: YES.. when will u get home?

Arthur: probably like 40 mins

Megan: good hurry

Arthur: Meet me over here at 9

Megan: shud I go round the back like usual

Arthur: no front is fine

Megan: wat about the neighbors

Arthur: fuck them

Megan: no fuk me ;p

Arthur: soon :p

It's 8:10 pm. Mary gets in the shower and turns the water to near-boiling. He sways under the water. After wasting enough water to hydrate a desert, he picks up the soap and washes. He recalls the photos Megan sent. He imagines sucking on Megan's neck while she apologizes profusely for calling him "cancer" in that text message. His dick stiffens a little.

He imagines her pulling his hand between her fleshy thighs and pushing his fingers into her body. He imagines her moaning into his ear, "Baby, I'm going to move somewhere cold so Xena can live in a climate better suited to her breed." His erection grows. It wags through the steamy air as he tugs on his soapy hairless ball sack.

She's kissing his collar bones. He pours conditioner into his palm and fucks his hand, picturing her squatting down in the tub, reaching between his buns and impaling his slippery asshole on her reformed-Nazi forepaw. She fingerbangs him vigorously. He sighs deeply, having forgotten to breathe.

He imagines her affectionately sucking his sack into her mouth with his dick lying across her face like a beached porpoise. He sees her eyes shining up at him with unconditional love, where there used to be disdain.

He rises on his toes as he cums, spraying what feels like a full quart of backed-up viscous boyslime into the base of the tub where fantasy Megan had just lustfully sought repentance.

He towels off and searches the dresser for something he can wear. Arthur's jeans are a little too generous about the waste. He slides one of the wife's baggy t-shirts over his head. The cotton feels super soft compared to the sequined top he was wearing earlier that day. He likes the shirt's graphic of a cartoon bear hugging a heart. He feels like he is wearing a cozy tent.

The wife's lone cotton panties would just fall off his skinny legs. Arthur's many plaid boxers are also too big. He steps into a pair of dark gray sweatpants, pulls the drawstrings until the waist looks like a scrunchie, and ties a bow. He slips his still wet feet into a pair of crusty runners and jogs into the kitchen.

The time on the stove says 8:46 pm. He had told Megan to come over at 9. He opens a baggy of lunchmeat from the fridge and sniffs at its contents. Turkey. He stuffs the bag into the pocket of his sweatpants and darts out of the kitchen, skipping past Arthur on the floor, on his way to the sliding glass door to the backyard. The curtains sway in the draft of the AC.

He pauses and considers his options. If he takes Arthur's keys and goes out the front door, they will jingle noisily in his pocket. If he goes out of the sliding glass door, he won't be able to lock it from the outside.

He turns off all the lights in the house and kills the TV.

"This should be interesting," he says to Arthur.

Chapter 28

Sheryl Thinks Some More

The neighbor boy was gone. Sheryl was alone with her thoughts.

When she had dragged Tom in here to interrogate him, she was on fire with righteous indignation. After seeing the boy's face look at the toe in transparent confusion, the fire was thoroughly doused. A chilling uncertainty replaced her rage.

She sat on the edge of the bed next to the severed toe (back in its baggy). Her vision shook as her head throbbed.

She thought about Cory, picturing him in his usual dress slacks, shirt tucked in – same walking bag of dad-isms and comforting consistency.

She had liked his predictability. Once every couple of weeks, her sleep would be briefly postponed by his advances. His hand would rub along the curve of her side. He would kiss her shoulder, letting her know it was time for a few minutes of average but functional lovemaking.

She would bring herself to orgasm with her fingers while he went through his routine of in and out, side to side, kiss here, kiss there. It wasn't passion, but it sufficiently forestalled their falling into a sexless marriage. It had always been enough for her.

She was abstinent when they met. She had no lingering memories to contrast with their tepid maintenance humps; no nostalgic recollections of late nights spent in a fever of drug-fueled, sweat-drenched, animalistic fucking; no lust-starved voice in her head whispering, "Pssst, Sheryl. It's like you're already dead."

Was having access to her body not enough for her husband? Did he want her to act out symptoms of desire that she didn't feel? Was she expected to scratch and bite like a coked-up high schooler? This wasn't that kind of household. She wasn't that kind of woman.

No, their unremarkable sex life couldn't be blamed for the appearance of a severed toe. If he was just having an affair, she might have been able to excuse that as the weakness of his gender – maybe encourage him to join a men's group at church where he could learn tools to temper his adulterous cravings – but Sheryl wasn't about to excuse a severed toe.

She had thought the toe was just too fu... *effed up* for Cory. It had been somehow more manageable for her to imagine that the neighbor kid was a budding sociopath. She had subconsciously wanted to believe that *all* this recent weirdness had been the kid's fault because it would vindicate the man that she loved.

She felt stupid for blaming Tom. What kind of a seven-year-old would hide a whore's earring in his neighbor's sofa? Where would a sweet little kid even get a human toe? She couldn't believe she had waved it in his face. She hoped he didn't tell his absentee mother about it.

The next morning, in a neighboring townhouse, young Tom awoke beneath the faded covers of his bed. His mom must have come home from her night shift and moved him from where he had dosed on the sofa. She had removed the polish from his nails, too.

He got out of bed and checked the table in the kitchen for notes. Sometimes she left him a note before she went to work. He saw some of her scrawls in blue ballpoint on the back of an unopened bill:

Morning sunshine,

I bought more milk so you could have cereal. Please don't use Mommy's nail polish. It costs money. Hope you have a nice day. Don't leave the neighborhood please.

Xoxo

Mom

She always ended her notes with some kind of parental imperative like 'don't forget to lock the door' or 'don't talk to strangers' or 'stay away from those older boys.' He liked it because it made him feel like she cared.

Chapter 29

Kim, Unchained (Continued)

Kim stood in the dark hallway holding the purse full of cash. She was unable to believe her eyes. He glared back at her from his spot in front of her apartment door. Even in the dark of the hall, she could make out the texture of his repulsive skin. He looked like the kind of creature that could casually kill a beloved family dog. He was by far the biggest Bufo toad she had ever seen.

"Shoo," she said, nudging him with the tip of her shoe. He begrudgingly hopped away. She entered the apartment and locked the door behind her.

She spun around her tiny apartment with her arms extended like a propeller and fell back on her bed. She reached in her purse, pulled out the wad of crispy hundreds, and threw them in the air. They hit the whirling ceiling fan with a loud thunk.

Twirling hundred-dollar bills descended on her from above. She laughed ecstatically. Her face hurt from smiling. She arched her back and writhed around on the cash covered mattress.

She kicked out of her jeans and peeled off her shirt. She unclasped her bra and flung it in the air (it landed on the lampshade). She rolled around in her underwear on the freshly fallen currency, softening the bills with her perspiration. Her skin, clammy from the walk home and white as a Tylenol pill, stunk of girl BO and the inky fragrance of green paper. She fell asleep with money sticking to her body.

When she woke up the next day, it was already well into the afternoon. Her irritating stock-ringtone was chiming from somewhere in her purse. She sat up. Hundred-dollar bills stuck to her back as she rummaged for her phone. It was her work. She answered.

"Where *are* you?" her manager Stacy barked into her ear. Kim looked at her new green paper bedspread and smiled. "*Kim?* KIM! You're late. Tess is covering your tables, and she is *not* happy."

"Yeah, I'm here," Kim finally said.

"Why aren't you at work? This place is a fucking madhouse."

"I don't work for you."

"I'm sorry, did I dial the wrong number?"

"Listen, tell Tess I'm sorry and give her my last paycheck to make it up to her. I'm done."

"It's not that simple, Kim," her manager began ranting. "God, you fucking young people think the rules don't apply to you. You have to put in your two weeks' notice before you—"

"But it is that simple," Kim cut off her manager in a level tone. "Listen to me carefully, Stacy. I get to choose whether to sell you my time. My time is no longer for sale. The end."

"NO, YOU LISTEN TO ME! I FU—"

Kim ended the call. A mockingbird chirped outside her window. Her tiny apartment was aglow with warm yellow sunlight. She felt like she had just elbowed her way out of a second womb.

Tits, she thought to herself. *Big tits*. She looked down at the money. *Tits and a car?* She did some quick math in her head – *first tits, then a car*.

Ever since high school, Kim had fantasized about dancing in clubs for a living. She had drunkenly confessed this to a friend once at a party. The girl had laughed in her face.

"Your chest is like a dry erase board, Kim. Guys can get that for free in math class," Kim imitated the girl's voice as she scrolled through a list of cosmetic surgeons in her area.

Chapter 30

Stripper Kim's Night in the Woods

Kim drags the man by his index finger into the parking lot of The B&B Gentlemen's Club. He presses a button on his keys. The headlights flash on his little four-cylinder truck. She lets go of his finger. Her big fake boobs jiggle as she clicks across the asphalt in her brazen porno heels. She helps herself to the passenger seat and looks out the back window. *Why is he just standing there?*

The man is looking up at the bright white moon, hanging out there in the cold apathy of space, mooning its earthen captor in an immutable show of noncompliance. He says a prayer under his breath and then hops in the truck next to Kim.

They head north in search of trees and dirt. The man dutifully observes all the traffic laws as they drive. His courteous turn signal usage remains uninterrupted, even as Kim hungrily stuffs her face with his cock.

Beneath the steering wheel, she growls with her mouth full. She coughs out his dick to look up at him with wild eyes. The saliva tethering her painted lips to his rigid penis shimmers in the flash of passing streetlights.

The man presses a button on his stereo. The processed drums of Phil Collin's "In The Air Tonight" becomes the soundtrack of the drive. She fucks her head on his dick like she's trying to kill it. His balls are swimming in her rabid drool.

Three minutes and sixteen seconds into the song, she stops blowing him, and they both go completely ape shit as the drum break hits and the bassline drops. He tucks himself back into his jeans, content to prolong the adventure.

They pull into the unlit woods of a nature preserve. He turns off the vehicle, killing the lights. The park closed hours ago, and the place is deserted. She is alone with this man in the woods, and there is no one else around for miles.

He hops out, walks around the back of the truck, and slides beneath the vehicle. Kim hears something metallic scraping and then clicking into place. He climbs back in and shuts the door. The back of his white t-shirt is caked in dirt. He pulls it over his head and shoves it under the seat. His chest is a mess of tattoos and scars. Elegant lettering spells out "Just mustard on mine, thanks" above his abs.

"What were you doing back there?" Kim asks.

"Fetching a joint. There's a little magnetic box stuck to the chassis," the man explains.

"Clever."

"Maybe," he says as he sets flame to the tip of the joint and sucks until it's evenly lit.

He exhales a plume of pot smoke so thick it obscures their vision. The overhead light turns off, leaving them in a cloud lit only by what moonlight falls through the leaves above. Kim sees an orange ember floating towards her and reaches out to take the joint. The oily paper sizzles as she sips in deeply, adding pot smoke to the taste of precum on her palette. She holds her breath for several seconds and exhales.

"I think I'm good on this one, buddy," she says, waving around the joint, unsure exactly where he is. She feels his hand wrap around hers, guiding it through the opaque cloud.

"You can just put it out here," he whispers. She pushes the joint against something that crackles. Suddenly, the truck cab smells like burning hair.

"What the *fuck* is that smell?" she asks through a fit of coughing.

"My burning nipple." He laughs the same laugh she first heard in that restaurant almost five years ago.

Chapter 31

Earlier That Night

About an hour ago, Kim was on her hands and knees, winking her asshole inches from the man's face. He was sitting by the poll next to a stack of bills, sliding them one by one onto the glowing platform.

She reached back and pulled his face between her asscheeks. She felt his tongue, chilly from the ice in his vodka, press against her butthole. This was met by whistles of approval. She grabbed him by the ears and theatrically wiped his face with her ass crack, bouncing to the music. A group of young people at the bar whooped and cheered raucously.

She felt him balance the remainder of his pile of cash on her lower back. She swept it off onto the platform nonchalantly and turned around, leaning over the rail to whisper a practiced line, "Do you want to get us a bottle and hang out in the back for a bit?"

He had whispered back, "I'm not crazy about champagne." He knew bottle service was a heist, but he wasn't dismissing her sales pitch, he was just being honest.

She had recognized his voice immediately. She pulled back to get a better look at his face and noticed the thumbs-up tattoo by his eye. Her jaw dropped. He squinted his eyes, inspecting the face beneath the makeup, and then his jaw dropped too.

"Holy shit, you're Kim the waitress! I didn't recognize your rectum!"

"*Shh*, don't say my name in here, you doofus," she hissed in his ear. "Stay here. I'll be right back."

She was flattered that he still remembered her name. This narrative had played out in her mind often, but in her masturbation fantasies, he still had that boyish late-teens look. He had grown into his features. He looked like a man now.

She crawled down the line of drooling men waiting to pet her until her song ended. She carefully stepped off the stage and then dragged him to the last cubby in the back room reserved for private dances.

She pushed him onto the sticky floor between the carpeted privacy walls. His back was against the bench. She put one foot next to his head, pulled aside her G-string, and fed him dessert.

She rode his face until she popped. When she dismounted, he had to mop his eye sockets with his shirt sleeves to regain vision.

"Fucking *hell*. Look at those new tits, Kim!" he screamed over the deafening trap music.

"You bought me these!" she said and mashed his face between them.

"LIFE IS SO AMAZING!" he yelled happily into her cleavage.

Chapter 32

Okay, They're in the Woods Now, and Kim Has Murder Tits

"Well, your fucking nipple smoke is going to make me sick!" Kim gropes around for the door handle and stumbles out of the passenger side door. A thick cloud of weed smoke billows out the little truck's cab. She kneels on the dirt, alternately coughing and laughing.

"Dude, why the fuck would you do that?!"

"Sorry, I guess I didn't think that one through." The driver-side door shuts.

They both get quiet. Dark, untamed woods surround them. The moon shines in shallow pockets of swamp. The dangerous dramas of nature play out quietly beneath a veil of omnipresent insect buzzing. Everywhere they look, innumerable species of plants are violently choking each other in slow motion.

"Wait, why are we in the woods again?" she asks, feeling increasingly paranoid.

"Hmm, good question..." he answers, scratching his chin thoughtfully. "We were back at The B&B, and you had just told me you bought those incredible tits with all that dead guy's money that I left you as a tip, back in that shit restaurant..."

He rubs his temples in an attempt to stimulate his memory, "...then I was all like, *holy shit,* life is so amazing because you were squashing me in the face with them... you said we should celebrate that we ran into each other again by doing something fun and crazy..." His face lights up as it all comes back to him, "...and then *you* said we should leave the club and go fuck in the woods somewhere!"

"Oh yeah," she coughs again, "I did say that!" she squints happily at him through a pair of bloodshot eyes. She slaps her hand onto his crotch. Just as she is about to lean in and kiss him, a red flag goes up in her head. Something he just said is bothering her, but she can't remember what. Then it hits her.

"What did you mean by 'all that dead guy's money'?" She felt suddenly uncomfortable and inched away from him.

"Oh that, yeah... I was a little guilty about keeping the money I took from this guy I killed. It felt like, I dunno, like *blood money*. I mean, the guy had a wife and son, you know? I saw you and thought, now here's a girl that could use a break and—"

"YOU KILLED SOMEONE FOR THAT MONEY?! DO YOU MEAN TO TELL ME THESE ARE FUCKING *MURDER TITS*?!" she screams at him, staring down at her implants in horror.

They spend a moment in pregnant silence. Finally, he looks at her with a serious expression and says, "*Murder tits?*"

Chapter 33

What's in the Safe, Cory?

Years ago, when Cory had purchased the safe, Sheryl had appreciated that he was taking precautions to keep his gun out of the hands of their child. The pistol had been a wedding gift from her father. He wanted his daughter to be kept safe in these "uncertain times." It did make her feel safe. South Florida is like a subtropic Sodom.

Until recently, she had never even thought about trying to get into the safe. It was stored snugly behind the little door of Cory's nightstand. To her surprise and frustration, she discovered that it wasn't a combination lock. It couldn't be opened with a key, either. There was just a little fingerprint pad next to two led lights – one green, one red.

That night at dinner, she put a plan into motion. She was going to get into that safe. She was going to get into it that night. If she discovered something vile, she would wait to confront him somewhere far from gossipy ears.

After loading his plate, she told Cory that it might be nice to hire a sitter on Friday night and go for a stroll on the beach, just the two of them under the stars. Aiden didn't mind. He was a late bloomer, and at his current stage of development, he was content to stay in his room with his video games.

Cory had begrudgingly agreed to the date. He could always tell when his wife needed emotional maintenance, and he knew from experience that it was easier to just give it to her and get it over with.

He was unaware that something had tumbled out of his safe when he had hastily stashed his little collection after hearing the doorbell ring while he masturbated. He was also unaware of how far his wife was willing to go to insulate herself and her child from his dark proclivities.

"Honey?" Cory asked, seeing that she had zoned out. She was staring at his hands as they cut into the juicy tenderloin.

"I'll get dessert," she said, after shaking her head as if to wake up her brain and smiling at him. Desert had consisted of ice cream, hot fudge, and her prescription sleeping pills.

"You're not having any?" Cory had asked.

"It is a wife's duty to watch her figure," she quipped. *What's in your fucking safe, Cory?*

Later that night in bed, she fought bravely through wave after wave of panic. Her husband snored beside her. The man was a deep sleeper even when he wasn't drugged. She listened to him make yummy noises with his mouth while he slept. *He's probably dreaming about his secret lover*, she thought contemptuously, *or cutting off pieces of someone's foot.*

She slipped out of bed quietly and checked on Aiden. The boy was motionless. He looked dead. Her heart beat even faster. *What if I gave him too large a dose.* She leaned over his mouth and felt his warm wet breath against her ear. She sighed with relief.

She re-entered the master bedroom and kneeled by Cory's side of the bed. She opened the little door of his nightstand, exposing the safe. She patted around under the sheet for her husband's arm and gently encouraged it to fall off the side of the bed. She took the same hand that she had held on so many romantic walks and pressed its index finger onto the pad of the safe. The red light flashed, and the safe made a little angry beep. She held her breath. She was sweating. She listened to Cory's breathing. It was regular. He murmured something incomprehensible.

This thing must not read fingerprints when they are upsidedown, she thought. Even her ankles were sweating. She let a few seconds pass before trying again with a revised angle of approach.

She gently twisted his hand, carefully rotating it and pulled the finger back. His foot moved. She froze. He snorted and licked his lips. She pushed his finger onto the pad again.

The green light illuminated on the safe. Sheryl released her husband's arm gently as the door of the safe popped open. The arm retracted, and its owner rolled over to face the other direction. He murmured something about shredded wheat. She held her breath again. A full minute passed before she let herself move.

She inspected the shadowy contents of the safe. In addition to the pistol and the box of rounds, the safe contained a crumpled envelope, a plastic baggy of what looked like human hair, five stacks of US currency wrapped with paper bank bands reading "$10,000" on each of them, and a folded menu from a restaurant she'd never heard of.

For a moment, she felt excited by the sight of all that cash, but the feeling soured. She tiptoed to the kitchen and inspected what she had found in the overhead light of the stove. *A bag of hair, really?* The hair was curly and red. The menu was from a restaurant in their town. She opened the envelope.

Polaroids. She gagged. She barely managed to suppress a bout of retching. What the *HELL*? The polaroids told a horrified Sheryl their gruesome story:

The first photograph showed a grown man's body laid out next to that of a small boy with a head of curly red hair in what appeared to Sheryl to be the kitchen of a restaurant. Both bodies were the sickening color of death. A weaselly looking man in an apron was smiling broadly at the camera as he mimed a chopping gesture above the dead child's neck with a cleaver.

The second photograph showed the photographer's blurry dick entering the purple, gaping mouth of the dead man. A familiar hand hovered in the foreground, making devil horns. Sheryl's sinuses burned.

The third photograph showed a pudgy looking man with a mustache doing jazz hands with the child's severed arms while his face contorted with laughter. He appeared to be dancing.

The fourth photograph showed the weaselly man carrying the child's torso down a hallway with exaggerated steps like a cartoon Santa Claus. Sheryl swallowed back an acidy tidbit when she saw the red pulp of the dead boy's amputated stumps.

The fifth image made her drop the photos onto the stove and start crying. It was Cory, naked as the day he was born. He was straddling the dead man's face. He had the dead man's genitals in his mouth. His eyes were closed as he savored the taste.

She did her best not to sob audibly, but it took a tremendous amount of effort. *You don't get to lose it right now, Sheryl,* her inner voice hissed at her. She composed herself, steeling her heart for the difficulty ahead.

She used her phone to photograph the address on the restaurant menu and then put everything back in the safe as she had found it and crawled into bed.

Sheryl was glad she asked Cory about their beach date before she had seen him sixty-nining a cadaver. *There is a special place waiting for your soul, Cory Prembach.*

Chapter 34

Megan Visits Arthur

Mary worms his way behind the blinds and flops out of Arthur's kitchen window. He lands in the dirt behind hedges that would benefit from a trim, gets up, and scans the backyard for anything with a pulse. Satisfied that he's alone, he turns and quietly pulls the window shut.

He sneaks over to the sliding glass door to double-check that it's locked. Nothing but his reflection is visible in the window; shutting the curtain and turning off the lights had sufficiently hidden Arthur from sight.

Mary's long pink hair is pulled into a tight ponytail. Arthur's wife's teddybear shirt is super comfy, but the sweatpants are already giving him swamp-ass. He treads lightly in Arthur's crusty runners through the grass to the side of the house and hides behind a lush hibiscus. There is a clear view of the sidewalk from his vantage between the houses. He waits. *Any minute now.*

Sure as shit, there she goes. Megan walks down the sidewalk towards Arthur's house, her braless tits flop beneath a red shirt that reads, "Send 'em back!" in bold white letters. Reading the shirt's xenophobic sentiment makes him feel weird for having jerked off to her in the shower earlier.

When she is out of sight, Mary runs to the fence and hops over it. Xena issues one sharp bark from inside. She comes bounding out of the doggy door towards the intruder. *Shit,* Mary thinks as the wolfish beast tears across the yard towards him.

He rifles through his pockets and rips open the lunch meat bag. Xena stops in her tracks and cocks her big head. She sniffs at the air. With meat in his hand, she recognizes him as the girl in the skirt who gave her the frozen steak. "Here you go, baby, have some tasty turkey," he whispers, tossing her the contents of the bag as he heads past towards the doggy door.

Meanwhile, at Arthur's house, Megan grows impatient. She rings the doorbell for the tenth time and then tries the door handle. It's locked. *Open up, you motherfucker,* she growls under her breath.

Mary slips out of the filthy runners and squeezes barefoot through the doggy door into Megan's bathroom. The bathroom smells heavily of perfume. An unflushed turd floats in a toilet full of bubbling urine. *Classy,* he thinks.

He walks into the bedroom. On the mattress, next to a wand-style vibrator, is what he came to find. *Eldorado,* he nearly says aloud. *Amo la marihuana.*

On a paper-plate sits at least an ounce of green shimmering bud. He picks up one of the nugs and sniffs. *Bless you,* Megan, *you sexy bigot.* He pulls a few loose nugs from the bag and puts them in his pocket. He tries to fluff the bag to hide his theft. He takes a few rolling papers from the little orange pack on the tray and folds them neatly, dropping them into his pocket with the pilfered plant matter.

Xena starts barking loudly outside. Mary inhales sharply. He hears Megan's voice from somewhere outside.

Chapter 35

Kim and a Killer

She steadies herself against the guy's truck and focuses hard. She was high as shit, but being alone in the woods at night with a guy who just casually announces that he once killed someone is enough to put anyone on edge.

"No, seriously, what do you mean that money was from a guy you killed? What guy?" Kim asked.

He doesn't know why he even mentioned it. Maybe he subconsciously felt like talking about it with someone. Perhaps he had wanted to warn Kim that he wasn't just some angelic financial benefactor. *Okay, man, just tell her the truth.*

"Okay, okay. I don't want you to be all freaked out. It's just kind of a long story, and my tongue is like, glued to the roof of my mouth. I wish we brought some water…"

"Tell me who you fucking killed."

"His name was Big Man, and he was *not* a good guy."

Her nerves are slightly pacified by his willingness to explain himself, but she still wants to hear the whole story. Stripping had given her a lot of practice at sniffing out creepers, and somehow this guy still seems like a good egg to her. There must be a reasonable explanation, or she wouldn't have been so easily wooed by his warm and loving vibe.

"What kind of name is Big Man?" she asks, suddenly skeptical. To Kim, 'Big Man' sounded like the name of a poorly developed villain from a smutty eBook. "Wait, was this at least in self-defense?"

"I'll tell you the whole story, but…" he makes sticky noises with his mouth to demonstrate how cottony it is from hotboxing the truck with her, "Do you mind if we talk and drive? I need to get something to drink. My mouth is like a desert."

"I'm not getting into that fucking truck with you. You just said you killed someone! How do I know you aren't a cannibal?"

"Because I killed one with a hammer for ruining my mom's life, and gave you all of his money."

"You can't be serious… 'Big Man' was a cannibal? I can't tell if you're fucking with me."

"I'm not fucking with you, Kim. The guy was despicable. Even so, I still felt sick about it. Ending another human being's life is so fucked up. You get this impending sense of doom that just doesn't go away. Giving away his money helped, but I still feel kind of haunted."

"That's some heavy shit." Kim slaps a mosquito on her arm. "Is that why you were getting wasted at the restaurant that night? It sure didn't affect your appetite…"

"I was just trying to distract myself. I kept thinking about the look on his face. I wanted comfort food."

"Why did you ask me to piss in your mouth?"

"I was drunk. Also, I thought you were cute."

"You thought I was cute, so you asked me to piss in your mouth… Do you even hear yourself talking right now?"

"I dunno, man, I was thirsty!" he retorts, sounding froggy from being parched.

"Well, that hasn't changed," she laughs at her own joke. He laughs too. The mood softens.

The distant buzzing of insects is a comforting blanket of sound. The moon reemerges from its veil of cloud. Its colorless light falls through the foliage above in haunting shafts of illuminated vapor.

He gives her a funny look. They both get quiet. She reads his mind and says, "You have *got* to be kidding me."

Crickets literally chirp.

It's not like she hasn't fantasized about doing it. Ever since she impulsively agreed to, years ago in that restaurant, she has wondered if she would have gone through with it. His perverted request had become inseparable from her liberation narrative.

Fuck it.

She takes off her heels and tosses them in his cab. She shuts the door a little louder than she intended to. The soundtrack of the woods pauses briefly and then resumes.

She puts a dirty barefoot on the bumper of his truck and grandly gestures for him to kneel before her.

This charismatic young pervert had given her ten thousand dollars without ever expecting reciprocation. He had been the catalyst for her transformation, a veritable map to a glorious treasure chest. Almost five years ago, she had told this guy she'd piss in his mouth. Now that she was about to do it, she felt silly for being shocked by the request in the first place.

Besides, it's not every day you get to pee in the mouth of a killer.

"Yes!" he says as he falls to his knees on the dirt beneath her. He kisses her pale kneecap and then tilts his head back with his mouth open expectantly.

"Close your eyes," she commands. He does so without debate.

She fights the urge to laugh at his facial expression. She rolls up the clingy elastic fabric of a dress designed to be removed. She is bare from her white pelvic bones to her muddy pink feet.

She lets out a stream of hot piss, thoroughly diluted from all the watered-down shots the club's customers had thought they were getting her drunk with. The splashing sound in his mouth changes pitch as the water-level rises to his teeth. When his mouth is full, she directs the remainder of her tank onto the dirt beside him, turning it to mud. She looks at the well of urine in his upturned face. Bubbles rise to the surface. *Is he gargling?* He shuts his mouth and swallows.

After watching him ingest her liquid waste, she can't help feeling like the ruthless ruler of these dark woods. She helps herself to a fistful of his shoulder-length blonde hair and wipes herself dry with it.

"You were saying?" she says, poking him in the stomach with a muddy toenail.

"Damn, I was hoping you'd forget the story thing, and we would just roll around in some lyme-diseasey deer shit fucking each other's brains out."

"You're a sick puppy..." it occurs to her that she doesn't even know this guy's name. "You haven't even told me your name yet."

He looks up at her with concern as he realizes the truth of her statement, "Oh man, I'm sorry, Kim. After all this time. I thought I told you for some reason. My name is Aiden."

Chapter 36

The Day Tom and Aiden Stopped Being Friends

Tom rang the doorbell of Aiden's townhouse. A brown lizard stared up at him from the rim of a planter. "What?" he asked it. He rang again.

Aiden's mom answered the door holding a coffee mug featuring a stylized depiction of Adam and Eve. She looked exhausted. She rubbed beneath her eye with her knuckle and looked down at Tom.

"Hi, Tom," she said flatly. She had expected the boy to steer clear of their home after she had interrogated him with a severed human toe. Nope, here he was.

"Hey, can Aiden come out and play?" Tom asked.

If he had told his mom about our little chat, the woman definitely wouldn't have let him come over, she thought. She feels relieved. She tries to smile at him.

"He's uh, still sleeping, Tom," she replied.

"But it's almost lunchtime," Tom pointed out.

"I'm not asleep." Aiden appeared behind his mother. He looked groggy but awake. "Mom, can I go out and play?"

His mom was too tired to care. She sighed and then said, "Sure, baby, but don't leave the neighborhood and don't go to Tom's if his mom isn't home." Tom wondered if it had been necessary to say this in front of him. It wasn't his fault his mom was never home. Well, maybe financially, but he had never had a say in the matter.

Within minutes, they were outside, throwing a tennis ball at the side of the clubhouse.

"Why was your mom so wrecked?" Tom asked.

"I dunno. I'm really tired too for some reason," Aiden mumbled, catching the tennis ball as it bounced back and chucking it hard at the wall.

"Did she get drunk with your dad?"

"No!" Aiden said defensively. The ball rebounded into the landscaping. Aiden ducked under a frond heavy with sprinkler water and reemerged with wet hair, looking irritated.

"Why not?"

"What do you mean, why not?" Aiden threw the ball hard at the wall. It made contact and ricocheted into Tom's hands.

"I don't know. They're grownups," Tom replied as if this explained the question.

"I never see them drinking," Aiden said, sticking up for his parents.

"Have you ever seen your mom naked?" Tom asked as he lobs the tennis ball into the air. Aiden shouldered him out of the way to catch it but missed, and the ball bounced off the concrete.

"No! Don't be gross, Tom," Aiden said with a disgusted look on his face as he ran after the rolling ball.

"Not even once, like in the shower or something?" Tom called after him, reveling in his friend's discomfort.

An elderly neighbor looked at Tom disapprovingly as she passed them on the way to her building. He stuck his tongue out at her right before the tennis ball hit him square in the head. The woman cackled and walked away.

"Ouch, you bunghole! That fucking hurt!" Tom shouted at Aiden, who had thrown the ball.

"Serves you right for asking me gross stuff about my mom," Aiden replied, smirking.

"Fine, I won't ask you any more questions about your mom," Tom said and spat on the sidewalk.

"Thank you," Aiden said grandiosely. He picked the ball off the ground at Tom's feet and forced it into the pocket of his shorts.

"Have you ever seen your dad's dink?" Tom asked, knowing he was pushing Aiden's buttons a little too hard, but unable to stop himself. Aiden replied by punching Tom in the nose and going home.

Tom stood alone in the parking lot. He touched his nostrils and looked at his finger. It was red with blood. *Someone's a little grumpy. Fuck you too, you spoon-fed motherfucker. I hope your parents die*, Tom thought bitterly.

He walked over to the car belonging to the elderly lady who had laughed at him. He opened the door to the gas tank, unscrewed the cap, and pulled on it until he broke the plastic connecting it to the car. He threw it onto the roof of her unit. *Fuck you too, you old bitch.*

Tom stopped going over Aiden's house. He spent the rest of the summer bored and alone, trapped in a townhouse full of his own whispering mind.

Chapter 37

Just the Two of Us, under the Stars

The beach was black. There was no moon. Cory privately wished he hadn't agreed to this date. *Nothing like a draining death march on a desolate beach to rekindle that spark,* he thought sarcastically.

His wife had been acting odd this summer. At first, he thought it was just more of the same infectious restlessness he had grown to attribute to her gender.

He understood women to be a helpless species of whiney invertebrates, trapped in a cycle of sperm-theft and self-cloning. He didn't hold it against them. They had a biological imperative to feed pieces of their breeding partner's soul to their sniveling crotch maggots until there was nothing left but a husk, emptied of boyish dreams, sucked clean of even the potential for happiness.

He had married Sheryl because she seemed like the least afflicted member of her gender. She didn't spend her time frivolously organizing photo-ops to plague relatives with on Facebook. She didn't lust after Hollywood's nauseating twaddle. She didn't belittle him in front of other men, and she had managed to yield offspring without taxing him too aggressively. She was as acceptable a specimen for partnership as he was going to get, and he knew it.

"Sweetheart, do you think we should be walking out this far?" he asked her, but the crashing of the waves obscured his voice.

"Did you say something, Cory?" she replied in a loud voice without slowing down.

"Yeah, the farther we walk out here, the farther we have to walk back!" he said, trudging through the sand behind her.

"Are you not enjoying being with me right now?" she turned to ask, struggling to hide the thorns of derision she felt tearing at the maimed flesh of her heart.

"No, I am. I always do, but I would enjoy being with you more if we stopped walking all this way and just relaxed," Cory said, trying to delicately bring her attention to the fact that they had walked to the middle of nowhere. Hardly anyone ever walked this far out past the popular beaches. Not to mention there was now at least a mile of sandy vegetation between them and the highway.

Sheryl stopped walking. Even in the dark, he could tell she had made an effort to doll herself up. *Jeez, how many times has she worn that dress? Doesn't she own anything else?*

"I appreciate that you want to spice things up with a little lovemaking on the beach, honey, but the spot we parked at was plenty private. If something were to happen to us out here, they wouldn't find us for days," Cory whined.

He studied her face. Something about the way she was looking at him was unnerving. Hard points of starlight shined in her dark eyes. Her mouth was a joyless horizontal line.

She reached into her purse and withdrew a small bottle of water and threw it at him. He picked it up off the sand and said, "Thanks?"

She reached into her purse again, this time retrieving an orange prescription bottle. Cory was confused. *Does she want to get high with me or something? This is new. Maybe it's Viagra? Ugh, I'm probably going to need it.*

Sheryl looked like she was about to cry. She tossed the bottle at him. Cory caught it and tried to make out the label. *These are the pills she takes when she's too keyed up about her imaginary problems to sleep like a normal person.*

"Why do you have these?" he asked, still not understanding what was happening.

"Because you're going to swallow all of them, and then I'm going to sit down and watch you die."

He started to laugh nervously but stopped when her somber expression failed to change. He said, "Very funny, Sheryl. What's this about?"

"When I found an empty bottle of wine under our sink, I wondered why you had hidden it. I had always thought you knew I wouldn't care if you had a glass or two of wine in our house. Even Jesus drank wine, for Christ's sake, I thought. Then, I found your little hussy's shower cap! *That* upset me. I tried to imagine a situation that didn't involve you secretly fornicating with some cheap slut. I tried to come up with an excuse for you because I loved you. Low and behold, one afternoon, I'm looking for the remote in between the cushions of our couch, and I find *this!*"

She pulled a hoop earring from inside of her purse and shook it at him angrily. The look of confusion on Cory's face changes into a grimace of condescension. He clears his throat and raises a finger for her to be silent before he spoke, "You bubble-headed monkey shit. You have *truly* lost it this time. I have never seen that shit in my life, Sheryl. I don't know what the *FUCK* you are even talking about. You are ranting like a batshit fucking democrat. You have officially lost it, you poor nutty bitch."

She nodded patiently, enduring his verbal abuses. She had expected him to lie so convincingly. After all, she had been married to this corpse-humping demon for more than a decade without getting a single whiff of his depravity. She pulled the gun out and pointed it at his face.

"WHAT THE FUCK, SHERYL?! HOW DID YOU GET INTO MY FUCKING SAFE?!" Cory screamed at her.

"I'm glad you recognize where this is from because there were a few other items of interest in that safe that I'd like to discuss."

She knows, Cory thought with dread and broke into a cold sweat. His guilt was infinite. *She must have seen the pictures, FUCK!* He looked at her with pleading in his eyes. Her cold facial expression didn't change.

"Give me my gun, Sheryl."

"*Your* gun? My dad bought you this gun as a wedding present to keep *me* safe. It's serving its purpose nicely, isn't it, *honey*?"

Cory took a tentative step closer. Sheryl stepped back and switched off the safety.

"Take the pills, Cory."

Cory started sobbing. He hadn't cried in several years. There was so much emotion trapped beneath the weight of his secrets. He cried so hard he felt like he was going to heave.

"Take the pills, Cory."

He sniffled, wiping a gelatinous tendril of snot onto the sleeve of his dress shirt. "Please, Sheryl. Have pity on me. I'm a sick man." He was shaking. "I don't want to go to hell yet, Sheryl!"

"Take the pills, Cory."

It was over. He had no fight left. He opened the bottle and took the pills one by one, sending each down with a sip from the water bottle.

She tossed a small legal pad with a ballpoint pen clipped to the top into his lap. He knew what she wanted.

In these final moments, he felt bottomless remorse. It hurt like nothing he had ever felt in his life. He saw with unprecedented clarity how mere exposure to his wickedness had robbed a loving woman of her warmth.

How many nights had they laid beside each other, her nestling affectionately into his embrace? He remembered her shining eyes when she had told him they were going to be a family. *My son! Oh God, our Son.*

He resolved not to let the boy grow up thinking his mother was a murderer. He took the pen and wrote the following:

Dear world,

I have been fighting a losing battle with mental illness. I have arrived at a point where I am no longer willing to go on. I am no longer willing to put my beloved wife and son at risk, should my condition further deteriorate. Please cremate this body. It has burdened the world enough with its presence.

Tell my family that I love them and that I am sorry beyond words.

Goodbye,

Cory Prembach

Chapter 38

Megan Comes Home

Xena is barking wildly. *Fuck, fuck, fuck.* Mary runs into the bathroom and pushes the flap of the doggy door just enough for him to peek outside. Xena is standing at the fence, barking at something in Arthur's back yard.

Megan emerges from behind Arthur's house and walks up to the fence. "Shut up, you dumb dog. It's just me."

Fuck, she must have gone around back when no one answered.

Mary panics. *Fuck, I'm wasting valuable time.* He decides to make a run for the front door. He bolts through a pictureless hallway into a living room with no furniture. *Wow, this girl does not know how to decorate.* He hurries out the front door, only to rush right back in. He had gotten a glimpse of Megan coming around the house. She looked upset.

He hesitates, backing up slowly down the hallway and trying to think. Up until this moment, he had forgotten about leaving Arthur's muddy running shoes on the pavement outside the doggy door. He hopes she hadn't noticed them. He hears the front door slam shut. *She's coming!*

Mary runs into the bathroom. He falls to the floor in front of the doggy door, but when he tries to pop his head out, the flap bops a returning Xena in the nose, and she lets out a startled yelp. He panics and ducks into the bathroom closet, shutting its painted metal door with a screech. *Ugh, I'm so stupid. I should have just unlocked the damn door and ran. Now I'm trapped.*

Xena enters and sniffs at the closet door, but when she hears Megan come into the bedroom, crying, she runs to comfort her master.

Megan collapses on the floor next to the bed. Xena licks her face. "STOP," Megan hisses, pushing the dog's face away.

Mary spies on her through the narrow slits in the bathroom closet door. The empty wire shelving digs into his back uncomfortably.

"Fucking Arthur. He is such a *cunt*," she says aloud. She vents in frustration, "This is the last time he fucking blows me off! I'm not some desperate booty call he can just toy with while his fat wife gets to have his babies and go to games with him. That's the last time I make plans with that cocksucker."

Xena licks at Megan's tear-streaked cheek. Megan smacks the dog on the nose and shouts, "Stop fucking licking me, dog! It's *gross*."

Mary winces. *It's not the dog's fault some poor woman's husband wasn't available to fuck you.*

Megan starts sobbing again. She looks at her phone and drops it on the carpet. She smacks herself in the forehead repeatedly. Xena tries to put her big doggy head in the way to prevent the blows from landing. Megan gets up in a huff and grabs Xena by the collar, "That's it, you're going in your kennel. I can't deal with you right now!" she shouts at the dog while dragging her out of the room.

This is my chance, Mary thinks. The closet door is stuck on its track. He tries to wiggle it free without making a racket. He feels it start to give, but when he slides it a couple of inches, it makes a horrible squeaking noise. He manages to shut it again just as Megan walks back into the room.

She sits on the bed and rolls a joint. She lights it. The smell reminds Mary of why he came. He pats his pocket. *Weed. I may be trapped in the closet, but damn it, when I get out of here, I'm going to get higher than a dwarven flautist's queef.*

She picks up her phone and begins distractedly, thumbing at her phone.

"Ugly," swipe.

"Ugly," swipe.

Megan blows out a plume of smoke.

"Ugly," swipe.

"Mexican," swipe.

"Ugly," swipe.

"Hey, boy," tap tap.

She must be on a hook-up app, Mary thinks. *This could be a long night.* He shifts slightly to try to get more comfortable. There just isn't space.

Mary watches Megan thumbing sexual solicitations into her phone. A half-hour later, the doorbell rings. *Yay*, Mary thinks happily. *I'll make a run for it when she gets up to answer the door.*

Megan tosses her phone on the floor next to the mattress and shouts, "IT'S OPEN! COME ON IN!"

Shit.

The door opens and shuts with a bang. *What's up with mouth breathers always slamming doors?* Mary wonders.

"Where the *fuck* are you, hoe?" a gravelly voice shouts down the hall.

"Calm your tits, fuckboy, I'm in the bedroom," Megan responds, putting the joint out and setting the paper plate of weed on the floor by the wall.

"Fuck you just say to me, bitch?" a voice snaps as its owner walks into the room.

Mary looks at the guy. *What a fucking juicer.*

Megan looks up at the pissed off chine of beef that just stomped into her room. She repeats herself, "I said: Calm. Your. Tits. *Fuckboy.*"

He punches her in the head. Mary gasps in surprise and slaps a hand over his mouth to stop any further sounds from escaping. *Holy shit, that escalated quickly. Is this how straight people date these days?*

Megan falls unconscious on the bed. Xena growls from inside her kennel in the living room.

Man, she knows how to pick 'em, Mary thinks. He feels like he should do something, but he isn't exactly white knight material.

The meathead tries to tear off Megan's jeans but can't get them over her sneakers, which further exacerbates his roid-rage. He slaps Megan's slack face and shouts, "I'm a fuckboy, huh?!" He hits her again and barks, "Yeah, I'm a *fuckboy*, alright, you junkie hoe. You invite *me* over, talking shit about *come fuck me, daddy.* I drive to your skanky ass house, and now *I'm* a fuckboy?!"

He grabs the neckline of her t-shirt with both hands and rips, exposing the jiggling breasts and belly beneath it. The torn shirt hangs off her sides like a jersey knit vest.

Mary's eyes move down from Megan's pierced nipples to the fading tattoo of an iron cross below her navel. *Wow, I called the Nazi thing*, Mary thinks.

The toasted gym-rat hocks a loogy noisily and then spits it in Megan's face. It rolls down her bruised cheek. He pulls hard on her pierced nipples and then punches her breasts repeatedly. Her eye socket is swollen, and her lower lip is split down the middle. Mary peers at the soft, exposed flesh of her body and hates himself for feeling aroused. *Get a fucking grip*, Mary. *This woman is in trouble.*

Xena's barking intensifies.

The skeevy juicer takes photos of Megan's exposed body with his phone. He violently rolls her onto her stomach. He spits on his hand and rubs his saliva between her soft and fleshy buns. He pulls down his black jean shorts (heavily embroidered with cheesy tribal designs in red thread) and starts yanking on his penis in an effort to wake it up.

His back faces Mary in the closet. *Even this guy's butt cheeks are spray-tan orange.* Mary finds himself wishing Megan stored swords in her closet.

"Fuck!" the beefy shithead shouts in annoyance at his inability to get hard. His elbow works frantically, but his penis doesn't share his mind's enthusiasm for rape. He decides to take out his impotence on Megan's motionless body. He starts squeezing her throat with his barbell-gripping bro hands. Mary's eyes dart around the room, looking for something to disable this beast.

Xena tries to chew through the bars of her kennel.

After a few mindless moments of angry strangulation, Megan's assailant steps back in shock and horror at the work of his own hands. He is shaking his head and quietly murmuring, "Shit. Shit. Shit. Not again…"

Mary can't make out what the guy is saying, but his body language is obvious. *Holy shit, did this asshole just fucking kill her?*

As the bulky orange beast backs away from the bed, Mary finally gets a glimpse of the thumb-sized snout of a flaccid penis head poking through a black bush the size and shape of a hemorrhoid cushion. A chunky pocket-knife falls from the pocket of the shorts bunched around the man's spray-tanned ankles as he waddles away from the bed.

Xena's cage bars rattle unceasingly. Her barks echo like gunshots through the sparsely furnished house.

"I'm going to kill that noisy fucking mutt!" Megan's strangler snarls and rushes from the room. He stops in the living room to pull his shorts up and then begins mercilessly kicking Xena's kennel. Xena yelps in alarm and then gnashes her teeth and growls defensively.

The metallic shrieking of the bathroom closet door sliding open is barely audible in the chaos of barking.

"AHHHHHHHHHHHHHHHHH!"

The goon whips around just in time to see a scrawny pink-haired waif screaming his head off as he takes a running leap into the air. The last thing the man sees is a faded T-shirt graphic of a teddy bear hugging a heart before the blade of his own pocketknife permanently opens his third eye.

The man falls against the kennel and onto the floor, his dead eyes twitch beneath the knife handle sticking out from his bloody forehead like a mythical horn.

"It's okay, baby," Mary consoles Xena and then shouts at the corpse, "You are a bad man!"

"Who's a bad man? What the hell is going on in here," a thoroughly fucked up looking Megan says in a croaking voice from the hallway.

"You're alive!" Mary says with relief.

Megan shrugs as she rubs her throat, squinting at him through swollen eyes.

"You need to be nicer to your fucking dog, lady! She *loves* you," Mary tells Megan. His blood is still surging with adrenaline, but he can feel himself beginning to calm down.

"Don't tell me what to do, fuckboy," Megan chokes out as she tries to steady herself and then slides onto the floor with her back against the wall. "Why are you…" she coughs and continues, "…you weren't this blurry in your picture," she says deliriously.

"I'm not here to have sex with you, Megan," Mary says as he releases Xena, who charges past him to lick Megan's face. "Fucking *stop*, dog," she says as she shoves at Xena's furry head and then looks up at Mary, "your profile s-s-specifically said that you weren't a f-f-fucking fag."

Mary sighs and picks up the blanket inside Xena's kennel. He uses it to wipe his fingerprints off the knife handle, trying his best not to get one-dimensional villain blood on in it. He rubs his prints off the latch of the kennel and then walks back to the bathroom and wipes down the closet door.

He picks up Megan's cellphone using the blanket as a glove and walks back to where she is seated. He pushes it into her hand and says, "Look, lady, you may wanna call the hospital or something. You look pretty hurt."

He drapes the blanket around Xena. She looks up, panting heavily. He winks at her before walking back to the bathroom. He crawls out the doggy door, slips on Arthur's sneakers, hops the fence, and crawls back through Arthur's kitchen window.

The living room smells terrible. He sits on the sofa and picks up the board game box from its nest of broken table shards and sets it on his lap. He breaks up one of the nugs in his pocket on the cardboard surface, unfolds the papers, and rolls himself a fatty. He sets the box on the floor. *What a crazy fucking day*, he thinks as he lays back and puts the joint in his mouth. *Fuck, no lighter.*

Mary falls asleep just as several vehicles pull in front of Megan's house. The blinds flicker with blue and red light as he sinks into a beautiful dream about being an armor-clad barbarian princess in a daytime television fantasy. His dream bangs look so fucking sexy.

Chapter 39

Aiden's Dad Passes Away

Aiden had loved his dad in the way he thought children were supposed to. This took the form of acting appreciative when prompted (by his mother, usually) and drawing pictures for the man on Father's Day. He never really bonded with him, though.

Aiden's dad had occasionally tried to talk to him about the important things in life, but the man's voice didn't hold his attention. There was something faintly off about their little father/son talks. They made Aiden feel awkward. In addition to making him uncomfortable, they were an intrusion on his playtime. In truth, he found his dad kind of annoying.

His mother regularly reminded him that his father worked hard so they could have a decent place to live. When that didn't seem to inspire appreciation in her son, she would remind him that it was his dad's money that bought all his toys.

Tom had begun to annoy Aiden also. He would come over uninvited and just sit there while Aiden played games. Eventually, Tom would get bored enough to go wandering around their house. Aiden sometimes overheard Tom talking to his mom about boring adult stuff. He once heard Tom ask his mom what she thought about Teflon pans.

Tom seemed so much older. Where were his parents? He was always talking about stuff from movies that Aiden wasn't allowed to watch. He also had an irritating habit of telling Aiden crazy stories – nonsense about finding dead bodies and hiding from bad guys. Aiden didn't think they were true, and if they were, he didn't want to think about that kind of stuff anyway.

Aiden was planning on finally telling Tom he didn't want to be his friend anymore. He just hadn't worked up the nerve. Then Tom started asking him dirty questions about his parents by the clubhouse, and Aiden had socked him in his annoying face. That took care of the problem.

Aiden's dad was always home on Saturdays. Usually, his mom would go out and do boring things with the crazy-eyed ladies from their church while his dad sat on the sofa watching TV. Sometimes he would knock on Aiden's door and say stuff like, "Whatcha doin', sport?"

Then one Saturday, things were different. Aiden walked into the kitchen, and his mom was standing there, silently staring at the empty coffee pot. The look on her face made him shiver.

"Where's dad?" he asked.

"Your father left me last night, Aiden," she said, not bothering to explain. The previous evening, Aiden had been at home with Julie, his babysitter. His parents had planned to have dinner and go for a walk on the beach.

He didn't know how to respond to his mom's statement. He walked up to her, wrapping his arms around her, but she didn't hug him back. She put her hand on the top of his head for a moment and then walked into her bedroom and shut the door.

Several days later, a police officer had come to their townhouse. His face was grave. Aiden wanted to play with the man's walkie-talkie. His mom told him to go to his room, but he eavesdropped on their conversation from the hallway.

The officer told her a runner had reported a dead body on the beach. They were able to identify the body as belonging to her husband. The officer handed her a folded note written on legal paper and explained that it had been in her husband's pocket.

The officer gave her a pamphlet and told her to call the number on it if she needed to talk to somebody about all of this. He apologized for her loss repeatedly and then informed her that Cory's body was available for arrangements. She nodded mechanically, thanked him, and shut the door.

When Grandma Pip died when Aiden was five, his mom had told him with tears streaming from her eyes, "She's in heaven now, Aiden. She's probably at a waterpark right now, going down a really fun slide!"

When the officer left, his mom sat down on the sofa and stared at her wedding ring for a long time. When she finally noticed Aiden peeking out at her from his room. She told him flatly, "Your father is dead."

Her face was empty. Aiden wept alone that night.

Chapter 40

Aiden's Story

"Aiden, *eh*? Well, it's nice to meet you, *Aiden*," Kim says, shaking his hand formerly, now that she knows his name, and pulls him to his feet. The knees of his jeans are black with dirt. His chin is still shiny from her urine. "Now who the hell is... *was* Big Man?"

"Okay, okay. So... Where do you want me to start?"

"The beginning, obviously."

"It's a long story..." Aiden warns her, waving an insect away from his face.

"Tell me!"

"Here..." Aiden helps Kim onto the hood of his little truck, where she can sit with her feet on the bumper, and then hops up, joining her.

"So, my dad committed suicide when I was seven."

"Oh my God, I'm so sorry."

"It's fine, really, but thank you," he turns to her with a hazy but sincere look on his face and says, "I'm not even sure you're going to believe any of this, but I want you to know that I try always to tell the truth. I feel like all of the fucked-up problems in this world wouldn't even exist if people just told the truth."

She can tell he means it. Working as a waitress and then as a stripper, she has met a lot of people, and one thing the vast majority of them have in common is this: They would rather say something untrue, no matter how fake and stupid it makes them sound, than be in a socially uncomfortable situation. People lie so much they don't even realize it.

"So, the thing is, after all the dust settled and the family came down, and we did the whole funeral thing, I found something weird. My mom was talking to a woman in the kitchen. The lady had brought us some gooey green bean thing she cooked because she felt bad and—"

"I feel like I've eaten that recipe before," Kim interrupts him.

A twig snaps somewhere nearby.

"What was that?" Kim asks.

"It was some kind of casserole," he responds and then continues, "My mom had left her cellphone in the bathroom…"

"Did you go in there to masturbate or to take a dump?" Kim asks, unable to control herself.

Aiden laughs, "I hadn't discovered that little pastime yet."

"You didn't know how to make shit yet?" Kim asks him, looking incredulous.

"No, I mean, masturbate. Where was I?"

"You were in the bathroom masturbating because you didn't know how to shit yet."

Another twig snaps.

"What was that?" Aiden asks.

"A dumb joke? I don't know. I was just trying to be funny, I guess," she responds. "What was so weird about finding your mom's phone in the bathroom?"

"It wasn't the phone itself that was weird. It was what I found on it."

"Did you see her naked?"

"Why does everyone ask me that?!"

"People ask you that?"

"Listen! What I found was just as scary," he said, ignoring her question. "There were a bunch of really aggressive texts from an unknown number threatening to drill a hole in her head, stuff like that."

"What the fuck, why?"

"I'll get to that. So, the texts from my mom said she had photos of them raping some kid's dead body."

"Holy shit, that's disgusting."

"My mom was out there having a calm conversation over coffee with some church lady, and meanwhile, I'm in there reading these texts she sent back to this person, and they are like ice-cold."

"How so? What did she say to them?"

"Well, the person texting her was crazy angry, but her responses were just super to-the-point about everything. She said some hard shit like, *come around if you don't feel like being alive anymore*, and then she blocked the number."

"Your mom sounds like a fucking badass."

"After my dad died, my mom was like a totally different person. She had always been really warm and loving, and then all of a sudden, she was like spooky. I guess she was trying a bunch of different antidepressants."

"Can you blame her, though? Her husband killed himself. That would be enough to fuck up anyone emotionally."

"That's what I thought, too. So, months go by, and my mom hasn't even started looking for work. I was back in school, and she was available to pick me up and drop me off every single day."

"Did your dad have life insurance or something?"

"No, I overheard my uncle asking her that at dinner after the funeral. She told him no and that she was going to start looking for secretarial work."

"*Good luck,* everyone wants you to have years of fucking experience."

"You poor thing."

"What happened next?"

"Fast forward a couple of years, and my mom *still* isn't working. She isn't even involved with her church anymore, which was—"

"I would have never pinned you for a good church-going boy," Kim teases.

"Yeah, we used to go every Sunday morning. The church was really important to her, and then all of a sudden, it wasn't. After the casserole lady, she pretty much ghosted everyone."

"Maybe she thought it was fucked up of God to let her husband kill himself when she a had kid to take care of."

"God doesn't work like that…"

"*WHAT?!* Are you telling me you believe in God? A stripper just drained her bladder in your holy host hole, bud. How are you a Christian?"

"I'm not, I just – wait, 'holy host hole'… I get it," he leans his forehead on her shoulder and shakes silently with laughter, "Kim, I think I love you."

"You and every other guy that walks into The B&B."

"Touché."

"Okay, your mom quits church and doesn't work. She was probably just collecting welfare and mad at God. Maybe one of your relatives was helping her out."

"Definitely not relatives – she cut *everyone* out of our life. She didn't want me hanging out with friends. She never talked to family anymore. She didn't even answer her phone when it rang."

"Yeah, really don't blame her there. Self-isolating is underrated."

"She started buying stuff, expensive stuff. Like, here's this unemployed single mother driving around in a fucking Benz. She would come home with all these boxes. She bought me like every gaming system ever made."

Chapter 41

Back in the Strip Club, Someone Was Asking Questions

Earlier that night, when Kim left the club with Aiden, she hadn't realized she was being observed. Back at the bar, a man asked a dancer if she knew the guy Kim was leaving the club with.

Bri responded to his question with a question, "Why, is someone a little jealous?" Her breath was heavy with tequila. It was nearing the end of Bri's shift, and she was trying to shake down one last dance for a quick buck. By this time in the night, most of the boys were either already broke or too drunk to feel the guilt trip she laid down when they refused to accept her advances.

"Do you recognize him or not?" The man asked impatiently.

Spooky fucker nosing around in a girl's business… He's fixing to nose around in his wallet, Bri thought.

"Conversation is for customers only," she clucked, in a tone that hinted she might know something.

Three minutes later, the man was sitting in a cubby in the back. Bri stood facing away from him. Her brown butt cheeks clapped audibly as she rose and fell on her heels to the explosive bass. She was taking her time, running up his bill. Every song is thirty bucks, and the DJ changes tracks like he has ADHD.

She accelerated her speed, and her whole body started to vibrate. The rippling skin of her heavily tattooed flesh was hypnotizing. Her ass flesh bounced wildly above her muscular legs. When the song changed, she turned around and climbed on the bench, a knee on each side, straddling his lap – rubbing up against him.

He could feel himself grow hard beneath her. She tugged on one of the yellow fabric triangles of her top, a heavy breast fell free, bouncing and swaying with her movements. She lifted it to his lips.

"Lick it."

He did. *Remember why you came here, you fucking pushover*, he scolded himself. She pushed him against the wall and propped herself up on one of her glossy yellow acrylic heels. She rotated her hips in his face. She pulled the narrow bikini bottom taut and brushed up against his mouth. She felt warm and soft on his chin.

His head spun from her heavy perfume. His cock rebelled against the fly of his jeans. A wet circle of precum formed on the fabric, betraying him.

She dropped onto his lap as the song changed and rode him to the beat. She put her arms above her head and twisted from side to side, slapping him playfully in the face with her free-hanging tit.

"What's the matter, you don't like how I taste?"

He took her dark nipple into his mouth and sucked. She alternated between bouncing and grinding on his lap. *That's right, stalker boy, keep sucking. I got shit I wanna buy.*

The song changed. He looked up as if to say something, but she mashed her boob against his face – silencing him. She freed its twin. She pulled her nipple out of his mouth and wrapped her hanging brown tits around his face and smashed them against his flushed face, cradling him in a feminine world of smooth skin and dizzying perfume. For a moment, his mind lost all contact with reality.

The song changed.

She draped her braids over his head. He felt safe in her fragrant cage. She let her tits drop from his face. She pulled aside her bikini bottom.

She moved one of his balled hands beneath her and withdrew the thumb, pointed it upwards, and slowly descended onto it. Her insides seemed unnaturally hot. She rose off of it and lifted his arm. His eyes were closed as she pushed his wet thumb into his mouth.

"Mmm, good baby," she cooed.

Tough guys like you are my bread and butter. You fuckers come in here stamping around all pissed off. Then someone gives your lonely ass a little affection, and you just melt, don't you?

The song changed.

She wrapped her arms around him, imitating a loving embrace, while she ground into his hardon. She breathed hot air into his neck. He pulled his thumb out of his mouth and put both of his hands on her butt.

The song changed.

His eyes opened. He looked up at her and then looked away. He said, "That's enough. I'm good," and began to lift himself off the bench beneath her.

"So soon? You're no fun."

"What do you mean soon? It's been like five songs."

"Ha! Try seven, Big Boy."

"Big *Man*... Big Man Jr.," he corrected her, the stupid nickname sounding too clunky even in his mouth, "You said you would tell me about the guy that left with your coworker."

"Hmm, I feel like I do know something about that. Maybe it will come to me after you buy me a drink."

"No fucking way. I already owe you like $150."

"Haha, try again, Mr. 'Big Man Jr.' You owe me $210."

"Fine, I'll give it to you, but who was that guy?"

"First of all, I find it fucked that you're still asking about Misty and her fuckin' trick after I just loved on you like I did. Second of all, fuck you. Pay me."

Big Man Jr. rose to his feet. His erection had deflated. He felt used. Drained. He pulled out his wallet. It took him an awkwardly long time to count out the money – he only had $150 worth of big bills, so he had to count out the rest in singles. He was left with eight dollars.

She took his money and said in a disinterested voice, "I've only seen him in here a few times. That boy looks like he needs a therapist. No, you know what? I'll tell you what he *really* needs, he needs a good friend like you," Bri pokes Big Man Jr. in the chest. "Why don't you run along and be the one to tell him to cut that fucking hair off his pretty head like a damn man?"

"Just tell me his fucking name!" Big Man Jr. snapped, tired of being toyed with by this woman.

"Don't you *dare* come around here talking to me like that."

"I'm sorry, I'm just tired."

"Aww, too much fun at The B&B? Cranky Man, Jr. needs a little R&R."

"Please, it's important. Just tell me his name."

"I don't fucking know. Pretty sure he sells, though. I think I saw him um…" she snapped her fingers and nodded at the remaining eight singles in his hand.

"Are you serious?"

"Serious like death, buddy boy."

He sighed, feeling defeated, and put the last of his cash in her open hand.

"Was that so hard, baby? Anyway, I saw him slip an ounce to Frank by the ATM a few nights ago."

"You mean Frank the old guy in the bathroom that charges me to use the fucking urinal?"

"That's the one."

"And that's all you know?"

"Get the fuck out of here, broke boy."

Chapter 42

Aiden's Story Continues

"You don't still play video games, do you?" Kim asks, a little turned off by his comment about 'gaming systems.' In her experience, guys that played video games didn't play life.

"Damn fucking right, I still play. I sell weed for a living, Kim. Did you expect a scholar?"

"Well, so long as you have a job, I guess. Sounds like your mom didn't, though, and she turned out fine."

"Did she? One day, she's out somewhere. I don't know where. By that time, she was just leaving me home alone. I'm… you guessed it, playing games. *Bang*, all of a sudden, I drop the controller and nearly piss myself."

"Why, did some twelve-year-old in Korea slay all your Minecraft sheep?"

"Someone was hammering on the door like, really hard."

"Oh shit."

"I pull a chair over to the door and look through the peephole, and there's this massive fucking tank of a guy holding a pizza box. Thing is, he's wearing a suit. I knew pizza guys didn't wear fucking suits."

"Fuck that shit."

"It gets worse. He starts yelling that he has a special delivery from Benvolio's. Obviously, I didn't open the door. I just tried to stay quiet standing on that chair while this fucking suit is banging away at the door, yelling shit about how tasty his pizza is."

"Oh my God, that's so scary."

"He starts screaming about how he's not making any more free deliveries, and the next time she places an order, it'll come with extra *red sauce*."

"Now that's a *PUN*ishment."

The woods get quiet. After an awkward moment, the din of insects resumes.

"Eventually he fucked off, but his face was like, burned in my mind. I brought it up to my mom that night, and she started pacing around mumbling to herself. She was almost as frightening as the guy at the door. Eventually, she pulled herself together and got my dad's old phone out of her bedroom. She showed me a photo of two guys in corny golf outfits standing on either side of this sad-looking beer girl. The guy on the left looks like a fucking squirrel, but like the kind you don't want anywhere near your kid's nuts."

Kim's laughter is cut short by a round of coughing. Aiden pats her on the back and continues.

"The photo was pixelated, but the big guy was definitely the meaty pizza guy. I told her that was the man I saw through the peephole."

"Mmm, meaty pizza," Kim says, distracted by an image in her mind of steam rising off melted mozzarella.

"I know, I'm hungry too," Aiden says, staring out into the woods.

"I'm not going to feed you a turd if that's where this is going," Kim's face curls in disgust.

"Oh, *hell* no, that shit is *not* for me."

Somewhere in the distance, something slimy falls into a swampy puddle with a plop.

"What'd she do when you told her it was the guy in the picture?"

"She told me to go to my room and lock my door, and then she left."

"You must have been so scared."

"I was terrified, but I was young too, so I didn't really know how fucked up things could get yet. She came home hours later in a shittier car with a bunch of moving boxes and just started packing shit up. She didn't even ask for my help. We left that night."

"Wow, that must have sucked."

"That was just the tip of the iceberg, man…" Aiden says, walking around the back of the truck to get another joint out of the little magnetic box stuck to the underside. He reemerges with one in his mouth and lights it. "Our townhouse was in a nice neighborhood. Not like fancy, but you know, pretty decent. She moved us into a motel. We go from being down the street from a golf course to living under a neon sign. Some of the shit I heard through the walls of that place alone would fuck a person up…"

"Damn."

"Yeah."

Chapter 43

Big Man Jr. Visits Frank

Bri tucked her tits away and walked off in the direction of the dressing room. *Not a bad way to end the night*, she thought as she thumbed at the folded paper in her hand. Big Man Jr. headed for the ATM. He felt dirty. He withdrew another two hundred. The atm fee was a staggering sixteen bucks.

He fed the vending machine one of the twenties and punched the code for menthol. A pack of cigarettes fell with a thud into the trough. No change. *Greedy fuckers*.

He slapped the pack onto his palm, peeled and tossed the wrapper flippantly. He put a cigarette in his mouth and pulled out a matchbook that said Benvolio's. He had inherited a trash bag of them. After lighting up, he walked into the men's room.

Frank was sitting on a stool next to a tray of cologne bottles with a hand towel over his knee, looking down at his phone. He was stacking shimmering cartoon jewels into neat little columns on the screen with his fingertip. He didn't look up as he grunted at Tim, "Evening."

The walls were red. The urinals were black. Big Man Jr. stood in front of Frank, waiting for the old guy to look up from his game. At this rate, he would be waiting for a long time. He cleared his throat. Frank's phone made tinny jingles and boops. Big Man Jr. cleared his throat again, "You want a lozenge for that cough, boy? Two dollars."

"Who do you buy your weed from, old man?"

"*Ha*, I don't sell weed. Do you party, son? I may have a gram or two for you and a special lady if you can grow yourself some fucking manners."

"I don't want your shitty coke, Frank."

Frank looked up at him. The whites of his eyes were as red as a puppy's dick. He was smiling broadly. One of his front teeth was missing a piece, "You're in a poopy little mood tonight, huh?"

"My um, weed guy isn't hitting me back, and Bri told me you buy from that guy with the long hair."

"Maybe I *um*, do."

"You know I'm straight, Frank. I just want his phone number."

"Do I, kiddo? I've heard you make peeps a few times, and I've sold you gum by the stick – that's not exactly a background check."

"I'll pay you."

"Okay now, maybe we do know each other a little."

"I just want his name and number."

"I just want $500."

"Come on, Frank, I don't have that kind of money. Bri fucking sucked me dry out there."

"Mmm, that's my future wife you're talking about," Frank crosses his eyes and pretends like he's jerking off. "It all makes sense now. I'll tell you what. I'm having a fifty percent off sale: $300."

Big Man Jr. pulled the $180 from his pocket and fanned it out. Frank looked at the money, shrugged, and took it. "What's your number?" Frank texted him Aiden's contact information and said, "You didn't get it from me."

"Of course not. Thanks, Frank."

Chapter 44

A Sheryl Story

During a final private viewing of her husband's body, Sheryl discreetly snipped off Cory's finger with a pair of garden shears so she could get into his safe again. The irony of her carrying a dead man's finger home in her pocket that night had not escaped her.

She mostly wanted the money he had hidden from her. She started thinking bigger when she felt the grip of the handgun in her palm again. It made her feel capable of anything. The other contents of the safe suddenly seemed like a blessing and not a curse. She would make these fuckers pay her to keep their filthy secret.

At first, she had tried to conduct her blackmailing efforts anonymously. Cory's phone was useless; he had kept it clean of anything related to the men. She didn't know their names, phone numbers, or addresses, but she did have some fucked-up pictures of them doing horrific things in a restaurant kitchen. It couldn't be coincidental that a restaurant menu had been with the other keepsakes in the safe. She knew it was her best bet.

She set up a PO Box under a false business name and paid to have its mail forwarded to a second PO Box at another location, just in case. Her letter had been brief and direct. It said she knew what they did and could irrefutably prove it. It said as long as they sent 10k to her PO Box once a month, they could continue their current lifestyle without interference. It said the amount and frequency of the payments would never change. It concluded by warning that a single late payment would be rewarded with a visit from the feds.

She drove to the restaurant to confirm its address. She was also just curious. She planned on mailing the letter through the post, but the place was clearly out of business. She almost backed out entirely. What was the point? Her letter would just get returned.

She sat parked in the parking lot for over an hour. She felt crushing disappointment. She had placed all of her hope in this insane plan. What would she do when the money in the safe ran out?

She swallowed the last gulp of wine in the thermos she had brought. She started drinking shortly after Cory's death, despite the advice of the doctor that had prescribed her antidepressants.

She stared at the front of the restaurant, willing some positive new development to materialize. Something about the place having an 'out of business' sign while the rest of the units had a 'space available' sign seemed odd to her. The sun went down while her car idled. She was drunk. At some point, she noticed a light go on behind the faux stained glass of the restaurant. Her pulse quickened.

She made a decision. With Cory's gun tucked in her bag, she walked across the parking lot and slipped the letter into the narrow mail slot. She leaned down to peer through it, but there was red fabric draped behind it. Before she could pull her eye away, a hand pulled back the fabric, and someone's eyeball stared into her own.

She had never run so fast in her life. The adrenaline and alcohol were a potent mix. She was not a practiced drunk. She sped home, swerving dangerously.

She shut and locked the front door. Aiden hadn't even looked up from his game. The volume was higher than she usually permitted, but she didn't reprimand him.

She went into the hall bathroom, turned on the shower, and threw up in the toilet. She pulled off her clothes and crawled naked and sweating into the bathtub, freezing cold water rained down on her back. She threw up again in the tub. She watched the yellow foam make the perilous journey from beneath her dripping chin to the drain.

Sheryl woke up the next morning in the tub. She was freezing. She must have turned off the shower in her sleep. She shivered as she wrapped herself in Aiden's towel. She wiped puke off the seat with a piece of toilet paper and flushed it.

She looked in the mirror. She didn't recognize the woman she saw. The woman's mouth was twisted into an unfamiliar grimace. There was no soul behind the woman's cold and joyless gaze. A change had taken place in Sheryl.

Her husband's last moments had shaken her deeply. In forcing his suicide, she felt she had committed an act more egregious than murder: She had forced a wicked but repentant soul to commit an unforgivable sin. She was like Eve looking through a lens of knowledge she could never unlearn; the garden was the same, but the trees had always been fake.

She reached into her purse to check her phone. There were two missed calls and one new text message.

Unknown Number: r u seriously trying to blackmail us Sheryl? We know where u live!!! If u so much as squeak we will drill a fuckhole in the side of ur skull and make ur brat sip his mummys brains through a fuking coke straw

She looked up from the violent words to gaze again at her reflection. The woman in the mirror wanted her fucking money. She texted a response.

Sheryl: How did you get this number?

Unknown Number: GOOD QUESTION BITCH

Sheryl: It doesn't matter.

Sheryl: Cory had some knickknacks in a safe.

Unknown Number: I WILL FUCK YOU WITH A KNIFE, SHERYL PREMBACH MOTHER OF AIDEN PREMBACH

Sheryl: A package containing my husband's keepsakes are in the possession of a trusted third party.

Unknown Number: So??

Sheryl: So, there are photos of you guys taking turns sexually abusing the dead body of a minor. Do you know what that means?

Unknown Number: ur dead. Worse than dead Sheryl. U are so fucked ic ant even explain it. U are going to pray to die. So fucking out of ur depth here woman

Sheryl: No, I'll tell you what it means. It means you will send 10k to the address provided on the date specified.

Unknown Number: poor Aiden

Sheryl: Drop by if you are tired of being alive. This number is now blocked.

Unknown Number: WAIT

The doorbell rang. Sheryl set her phone on the sink and picked up the purse containing the gun. She walked out of the bathroom, wrapped in a towel.

"Are you okay, mom?" Aiden asked, standing at the entrance of his room. He looked sleepy.

"Aiden, play one of your games. Your mother's busy," she said on her way to the door.

She looked through the peephole. It was Gale from church. The woman was holding a large covered corningware dish with a potholder.

"Hi Gale, hold on while I get dressed. I just got out of the shower," she said through the door.

"Don't rush, sweetheart. I'm not going anywhere," the woman responded.

Sheryl quickly dressed and invited the woman in. Gale had cooked a green bean casserole for them. She hadn't been able to come to the funeral and wanted to give Sheryl her condolences in person. She also wanted and to tell her that she and Aiden were in her and her husband's prayers.

Sheryl made coffee and sat with the woman for a while. The two of them spoke in hushed voices.

Aiden walked into the bathroom and closed the door.

Chapter 45

That Thing in Fort Lauderdale

When those pictures were taken, they had all been drunk except for Cory. It was one of their happiest memories. They were celebrating a disaster averted. Greg had nearly gotten himself caught while hunting down in Fort Lauderdale.

A substitute teacher had been interviewed on the news:

"I got called yesterday to come sit in for Mr. Codner's tech class. That was my only class, so when the lunch bell rang, I dropped off my pass at the administration office and started to walk home. I saw a student talking to this kind of heavy guy with a mustache by the picnic tables. I thought, *wait a second, I know that kid*. Nicky's a good kid. I've had him in other classes. I dunno, the situation just felt wrong. When they saw me staring at them, they both waved all friendly, so I thought it must be his dad or something, and I just left…"

After the interview, the news anchor went on to say the police were now searching for the boy. Then a shitty drawing of Greg based on the teacher's description was shown, and viewers were asked to call the police if they knew anybody that looked like the man in the drawing.

Dillon dropped his spoon into a bowl of purple milk and spat out a mouthful of partially chewed fruit loops. Tiny droplets against the screen of the old TV sitting on his kitchen table. He immediately called Greg to warn him.

Greg hadn't invited Dillon to the restaurant in months. He had determined that three was the perfect number for his little get-togethers. It just felt like they ran smoother that way.

Lately, Cory had been much more interesting company. Dillon was just an aging pervert. Cory was downright dark. He was also far less conspicuous. They referred to Cory as Mr. Rogers behind his back because he came off as being so wholesome. Dillon was the diametric opposite of wholesome.

When Dillon called to warn Greg that he was on the news, the kid was still alive. He had been heavily sedated and locked in the bathroom of Greg's restaurant. Big Man and Cory were already on their way over with some groceries. The three of them planned on an afternoon of unbridled cruelty followed by an expertly prepared dinner.

It was a Monday morning. The restaurant was closed on Mondays. There just wasn't enough business to justify paying the staff. Having the restaurant empty on a weekday also accommodated Big Man and Cory's schedule; their wives assumed they were at work.

Their plan was fucked now – probably their little club, too. Greg wouldn't go down without a fight, though. He told Dillon to find out where the teacher lived. Dillon did that and more.

Dillon camped out in the bushes by the teacher's door. It wasn't boring, though. The bushes were full of beautiful things that he had never taken the time to look at it. There was a fuzzy caterpillar with a funny walk. A spider was linking glistening strands of web to the dewy leaves. Ants navigated a labyrinth of mulch. The time passed quickly.

He saw the teacher walking down the sidewalk in the distance and checked his watch – it was 12:23 pm. He shifted his focus to the task at hand. He pulled the stun gun out of his pocket and rested his thumb on its worn gray button.

The teacher didn't have a chance. Before he could close his front door, Dillon was upon him. After a crackling jab from the stun gun, the teacher was a sweating, immobilized heap on the tile. Dillon shut and locked the door, briefly peeking out the peephole to check for nosy neighbors. There were none.

Dillon removed his shoes on the mat and approached the man wearing socks. The teacher was hyperventilating. His body shook violently. Dillon removed his cloth belt and looped it around the man's neck. The teacher tried to resist. Dillon placed the sparking prongs of the stun gun against the man's temple and depressed the button for several seconds. The man's body flopped on the tile.

Dillon returned his efforts to tightening his belt around the man's neck. The face below him cycled through increasingly dark shades, settling on raisin purple. Pinpricks of red bloomed on the whites of the man's eyeballs.

That's when Dillon had noticed it: Hanging on the wall above an elegant gold-leafed console table was a framed *I love Lucy* poster. There were scented candles neatly arranged beneath it. To the average person, it would have looked like a shrine. To Dillon, it looked like hope.

He looked back at the shrine's owner. *Dead as dinner.* He walked through the man's house. He didn't hate the décor.

He felt something rub against his leg. *Fuck.*

It was a lovely orange cat. He watched as it sashayed to its owner's body. It touched the man's cheek with a hesitant paw. It then climbed onto his face and sat upright, butthole presumably pressed against the man's lips. It meowed at Dillon.

"Sorry, kitty. Your buddy was a rat. Nothing personal."

The cat meowed again.

"Yeah, life is like that, though, ain't it?"

A laptop was open on the kitchen table. Dillon opened cabinets using the corner of his shirt to cover his hand. He found plastic wrap, peeled off a sheet, and carefully carried it to the laptop. He wrapped the keyboard and touchpad. It was a little challenging to navigate the touchpad, but he wasn't taking any chances.

He checked the man's browser history. Celebrity gossip websites, Facebook, news... *The guy must use a private browsing tab for porn. Damn.* He closed the browser.

He ran a search for image files. The window populated with every image on the man's computer. Glowing before him was the holy grail he was seeking.

There were hundreds of selfies featuring the man dressed up as a woman. He was too masculine to be passing, but that apparently hadn't stopped him from playing dress-up in private.

Dillon called Greg.

"Tell me it's good news, Dill," Greg's voice said, sounding worried.

"Oh Greg, baby, it's a winning fucking lotto ticket."

"Did you find out where this rat fuck lives?"

"Yeah, I'm in his place. Kind of a fun vibe. Feeling like I just killed a likable dude."

"Oh shit, he's dead? Is there a mess? Big and Mr. Rogers are like ten minutes from the offramp."

"No worries, this shit was clean. Did him with my belt after a good zap. Even took off my shoes."

"Big and Cor are coming with one of the kid's socks. Shove it under the sofa."

"Will do. I found something that will distract people from that drawing of you in the meantime…"

"Music to my fucking ears. What did you find?"

"This guy has a fucking *I Love Lucy* shrine in his entryway and a fuck-ton of photos of him wearing dresses on his laptop."

"WE GOTTA GET THAT SHIT ONLINE, DILL!"

"Yeah, I'm on it. He's got a garage, too. We'll be able to load the body in private."

"What about his car?"

"He fuckin' walks to work in *this* heat. Probably some DUI cases. I'll check the garage, but I think we lucked out."

Dillon located the garage door and opened it with his shirt to check for vehicles.

"Fuckin' nada," he told an elated Greg. No car. No mess. No problems.

"Dillon, I want you to know that I love you," Greg said. Dillon could tell the man was smiling.

"Hasn't felt like that lately, Greg."

"From now on, I call you when I catch ANYTHING."

"You fucking bet you do. I'm stuffing today's little turkey, that's for damn sure."

"Does the guy have any Facebook shit you can diddle with? You know, make him seem stalkery…"

"Yeah, but it's not like I can just send the kid a friend request. Everything is timestamped on that fucking website."

"Good point," Greg said, pausing to think, "What about some travel websites? Make it look like he's running – search for shit about the Mexican border. Do Canada too. Make it look like he wants to know what to expect. Like, if they'll search his car or whatever."

"Perfect. Okay, I'm gonna hang up. Gotta get that address to the boys."

"I can't thank you enough, Dill," Greg said sincerely. The relief in his voice was unmistakable. Dillon hung up and texted the teacher's address to Big Man.

He opened a browser window and searched extensively for information about the property search protocols at both the Canadian and Mexican borders. He also researched what chemicals could dissolve human bones. He already knew this information, of course, but he wanted the search queries to be in the man's browser history during the inevitable investigation.

He looked through the drag photos and settled for an image of the teacher in a lavish emerald ball gown. It was the only photo of the man not smiling. Dillon knew the photographs were just innocent fun, but the fearmongering press would have a field day.

He opened up a private browsing tab and used a VPN website to hide his IP address so he couldn't be tracked. He created a dummy email account. He pulled the contact info off a couple of local news websites and sent them the image with a brief note: *My coworker is not who you think he is.*

He smiled. He wrapped his hand in the plastic wrap he had used to prevent fingerprints on the keyboard. He closed the browser and shut the laptop. He pulled out a kitchen drawer and emptied its contents on the floor. *Possible signs of struggle?*

His phone buzzed. It was Big Man, pulling into the neighborhood with Cory in the Lincoln. Dillon opened the garage door and closed it behind them.

While Big Man and Cory loaded the body into the trunk, Dillon slid the boy's sock under the teacher's sofa. He grabbed his shoes and the teacher's phone. He called 911. When the operator answered, he screamed *help* through the palm of his hand in a girly voice. He dropped the phone without ending the call.

On his way to rejoin the others in the garage, he spotted an old polaroid camera – the kind that ejects a square print of the photo right after you take it. He hadn't seen one in a decade. He grabbed it and joined the other two in the garage. Big Man and Dillon hid in the back seat while Cory drove them out of the neighborhood. They figured if anyone saw them and described Cory, the resulting police sketch would look like every wasp in the county.

Later that afternoon at the restaurant, they passed around a bottle of Gin. The mood was light. Dillon pulled one of the teacher's socks off to roll into a ball and chuck at Cory. He laughed when he noticed the teacher's cerulean blue toenails. Across the table, Cory was standing with a sharp pair of shears. He stared at the corpse's painted toes. His exhausted genitals stirred once more.

The following day, Greg's employee texted him to let him know that he had found a camera in the kitchen. He said he put it next to the register. The cook was in the country illegally, but his English had gotten a lot better since the day Greg had hired him. Greg liked him because he wasn't nosy, and he didn't have to pay him much.

Greg's heart jumped in his chest when he read the text. They must have forgotten the camera after they scrubbed the place down. *Who has those fucking photographs?* Greg thought in a panic. He raced over to the restaurant.

His waitress Gigi muttered hello to him in her usual unsubscribed tone. He knew she fantasized about quitting every day. Business was so slow he had to pay her a couple of extra bucks an hour to make up for the lack of tips.

There were two women from out of town sharing an order of garlic knots at a table in the far corner. They looked like they were regretting their decision to stop in for lunch. The food was okay, but the smell of cleaning chemicals was so strong they felt like they could taste it. The tragic mewling of The Righteous Brothers coming out of the jukebox was not helping the situation.

He walked to the register and picked up the camera. There were no photos. He breathed a sigh of relief. He walked into the kitchen to thank Moses for telling him about the camera, but the cook wasn't in the kitchen. He popped his head out the back door. Moses was smoking a cigarette by the dumpster. Dance music bled from the cook's headphones. Greg shrugged and left.

When he was back in his car, he phoned Big Man.

"Hey, Greg," Big Man answered.

"What did we do with the polaroids?"

"Fuck. I forgot about those."

"I was really hoping you had them."

"They weren't there when I left. I double-checked the whole place for… residue. I would have seen them."

"Well, we both missed the camera. It was next to the sink."

"Fuck."

"Yeah, we can't get sloppy, Big."

"Dill is gross, but he's not stupid. I doubt he took 'em. He knows I would fuck him up over some shit like that."

"Mr. Rogers?"

"That churchy fuck was finally starting to grow on me."

"Hate the swing, not the golfer."

"Would you stop bringing that up? He got lucky. My old putter was a piece of shit. It was fucking up my short game."

"Blame the equipment," Greg said, momentarily distracted by the joy of teasing Big Man about Cory killing him on the course recently.

"If that motherfucker took those photographs, you know he's busting a nut to them right now. That guy has been fucking the same old box since the Clinton administration."

"Yeah, you're probably right. He's so cautious about everything anyway. In all the years we've known him, he has never even invited us to that comfy little townhouse of his. I doubt the pictures are a real threat. He's so meticulous. I just don't like loose ends."

"Want me to call him?"

"No, he gets all pissy about his phone. That's what I mean. He's cautious. I'll send him an email about it and let you know when he gets back to me. I guarantee he will tell me he destroyed them either way. In the meantime, get that girl at your office to scrape up some info on him. Find out about that frigid little wife of his too. Just in case it ever comes to that."

"Good idea. Hey, did you see the news?"

"I checked this morning, but I didn't see anything," Greg responded, his anxiety returning with the memory that he might still be a wanted man.

"Check your texts when you hang up. You're gonna love this shit."

Shortly after they hung up, Big Man sent Greg a photo of his TV screen. The news station was running a picture of the teacher wearing a dress above the words, "Sexual predator fakes Nicky Beracola abductor story to throw off authorities…"

Greg laughed so hard he farted.

Chapter 46

Big Man Pays the Cannibal Tax

After Sheryl blocked Big Man's burner phone, he and Dillon had taken turns driving by her townhouse.

The kid never came outside by himself. They saw Sheryl drive him to school once, but seeing her in person made them feel less confident. She looked unhinged, which seemed to add legitimacy to her threats. As the end of the month approached, their cockiness faded.

What if she had been telling the truth? Big Man imagined what it would be like for Lidia and Jr. to see their father on the news. Dillon imagined what it would be like to shower in prison as a known child predator.

In the end, paying the woman seemed like the only real option. Dillon was not as financially stable as Big Man. With all of Greg's cash stashed away, in addition to his thriving law firm, Big Man was more than capable of making the payments. His quality of life wasn't significantly affected, but being taxed by a single mother gnawed at his pride.

Chapter 47

A Worldlier Sheryl

Sheryl pickled in her damnation. She ran from her God and church into the open arms of commodity fetishism, trying to fill the hole in her soul with shoes; when those failed to plug it up, she jammed in a shiny new Mercedes.

Her doctor had slapped a fresh pharmaceutical bandage on her wounded psyche, introducing her to various prescriptions until she found a functional cocktail of fuck-it.

She was a different woman. She used to call members of Congress about prayer in school. She used to picket women's health clinics. She used to include a bag of cookies in lunches she packed for her husband. Now she carried a Barretta when she shopped for handbags. Now when she thought about the afterlife, she took a Xanax.

At some point, buying things was no longer enough. She started picking up wayward boys from the local Christian college.

The first boy had just sort of happened.

She was driving around listening to secular music, feeling empty. It had been years since the last time she had received Cory's mediocre sexual ministrations.

She didn't hate men. She had lost the compacity for emotions as strong as hate. She just didn't want to tend to one like she had her husband.

Up until this point, she still thought from a framework that associated sex with love. That night driving around, a red lightbulb had popped in her brain. She had an epiphany: She was doomed anyway, fornication was now on the menu.

She parallel parked her car in front of a little hole in the wall bar. She turned heads when she walked in, not because of her appearance or her expensive clothing – this wasn't like one of those commercials pitching the notion that female empowerment is attained by wearing the right sweatshop-manufactured clothing. The kids in the bar were only staring at her because she was as old as their parents.

After she ordered a glass of wine, they inexplicably lost interest, and the bar resumed its usual din.

She told the bartender to bring a beer to the timid looking blonde boy at the end of the bar. When the bar girl brought him the beer and told him who it was from, he looked up from a library copy of Kierkegaard's "Fear and Trembling" with a confused expression.

She just stared at him like a lizard. It occurred to him that saying thank you was the polite thing to do. He put his book in his backpack and relocated to the stool next to hers.

They talked. He told her that the kids at the Christian College weren't allowed to drink, so this bar was kind of their hideout. He told her the patrons always got nervous when someone older walked in because it might be a member of the school's faculty.

Sheryl asked him if he thought she was faculty. Faculty wasn't allowed to drink, either, he told her, pointing at her wine glass. She asked him if he'd ever had his cock sucked. He blushed and said that it had almost happened at a summer camp he had attended, but he and the girl had gotten nervous and prayed instead. She bought him another beer.

After he finished it, she paid the tab. She told him she owned the Mercedes in front of the bar and that she would park it behind the building. She told him to wait ten minutes and then find her. He looked terrified. She got up and left.

He walked around the back, swaying a little bit, intending to tell her thanks but no thanks. When he got in the car to talk to her, she pulled onto the street and drove.

She was listening to classic rock. He felt uncomfortable. She put her hand on his thigh and squeezed. His body, longing for this forbidden affection, responded immediately by inflating his pious penis. His erection pressed uncomfortably against his khakis. She petted it lightly to keep him trapped in his helpless state of lust, but she didn't want him squirting out all his enthusiasm just yet.

She parked outside of a motel she would never dream of staying the night in. She put a finger on his throbbing cock and pushed it down, telling him, "Sit tight. I'll be right back."

He was still there when she returned with the room key. His forehead was glossy with the evidence of youthful terror. She opened his door and said, "You can leave now, but once we go in here, there's no turning back." He hesitated and then followed her into the room.

"Get in the shower," she instructed him as she unzipped her black skirt. He stared at her, full of fear and trembling, and then did as she asked.

The bathroom mirror was opaque with steam. The base of the plastic shower curtain was orange with the beginnings of mildew. Sheryl pulled back the curtain and stepped behind the healthy but shaking young college boy. She had removed all but her eight-hundred-dollar blouse, with its ridiculous puffy ivory sleeves. She looked like a Shakespearean actor except instead of tights running up to a sock-stuffed Barbie doll crotch, her pasty legs led up to an untrimmed bush the color of rust.

When he felt her presence behind him, he stiffened in more ways than one. The water had soaked flat the short blonde fluff of his good-boy haircut. His body was sturdy and upright but not especially muscled. He was lean. His bathing suit tan left his two fury butt-cheeks as white as his conscience had once been.

The beers had made him socially pliable but not drunk. She may have been softened into something more desirable through the lenses of his buzz, but not so much so that he managed to escape being fully aware of his situation. The red wine, on the other hand, had only made her a more pronounced flavor of callous.

She leaned up against his back. She wrapped her long fingers around his unblemished hips and pulled him against her. He felt her pubic hair flatten against him. She licked water off the back of his clean-cut neck. It tasted faintly of hair gel. She could feel his accelerated heartbeat drumming through his back.

He turned his head to look at her, but she raised her hand to his chin and firmly redirected his face towards the tile wall. He began murmuring something. She pushed her fingers into his mouth and played with his elusive tongue. She felt him push against her subtly, tentatively. His body was staging a mutiny against what must have been a torrent of moralizing thoughts.

Her ivory blouse was soaked to her skin. She reached her hand between his legs and tugged on the hair of his scrotum. His hand reached back, intending to explore her body, but she took hold of it and authoritatively planted it on the wall. She did the same with his other hand. He was in the position to be frisked.

She handled him without restraint. She played with his wet virgin balls. When she was bored of squeezing his testicles, she took hold of his rigid cock. *What the fuck?* She thought, totally shocked, even in the coma of her apathy, comparing him to memories of her dead husband. The thing in her hand was a fucking log. He was a baby in his twenties fitted with the cock of a bear.

Cold veins of understanding spread through the grassy fields of his naivety. She was older than his teachers, but the feeling of her hand gripping his cock was enough to blow the lid off his moral imperatives with a geyser of suppressed lust. For the first time in his life, he understood that he was an animal. He turned around and took control.

Sheryl was suddenly confronted by years of a young man's suppressed sexual frustration. He pushed her against the blackened grout and fiercely groped her sagging breasts through the soaked fabric of her ludicrous top. He tore it off of her, revealing the glary nakedness of her thoroughly lived-in body. Drops of water rolled down her chest as it rose and fell.

He squeezed the pale flesh of her stomach before seizing a fistful of her pubic hair like the nape of dog's neck, taking hold of her in a gesture of uninhibited dominance.

He pushed his nose into the loose wet skin of her neck and inhaled the faint ghost of her imported perfume. He sucked hard on her weathered earlobe and spat her earring on the bathroom floor. He pushed his tongue into her ear canal. Her nipples were so hard they hurt.

The hot water ran out. Frigid water fell through the steamy air. He kicked the handle, and the water shut off abruptly. He backed out of the tub. The look of animal intensity abated slightly. He stood naked, breathing heavily, and as he tried to process the feeling of being taken over by two hundred thousand years of animal instinct.

She pressed her open hand against his chest, forcing his dripping back against the peeling paint. She sat on the plastic toilet lid. His stupidly massive penis was so hard it looked like the skin would tear. She had never seen a boner like the one attached to this boy. It was like a hairy meat cannon staring her in the face with its pouting pink urethra, daring her to drown herself with the contents of the tortured vascular ball-sack dangling beneath it.

She sucked it. The swollen dick head in her mouth felt like it had a fever. The crazed animal again took residence behind the boy's bright, youthful eyes. He grabbed her by the chin, running the fingers of his other hand through her wet hair, taking hold of her skull and penetrated it mercilessly. She felt like her jaw was going to dislocate. She pushed against his firm stomach with her hands, fingers spread wide. He fucked her head, groaning unselfconsciously.

His breathing slowed to a halt as he came dangerously close to busting. She imagined her stomach filling with his cum like an old wineskin. She detached her head from his twitching cock before it could pop, stood, and turned to straddle the toilet, pushing her hands flat against the wall on either side of the faded floral print that hung there. She waited just long enough to abort his orgasm before it reached its third trimester.

"Put it in me." Her dry words were empty of music.

It took him a few clumsy jousts at her pubey openings before his cock was wearing her body. She felt like she was wrapped around a hot pipe. Her vagina felt stretched in a way she hadn't experienced since giving birth. The ironic image of a child's sock on an adult's foot came to mind before it was drowned in a wave of blinding sensation.

He started humping her. He didn't know what the fuck he was doing, but he was doing a lot of it. Soon she was slamming against the wall, gasping for air and moaning like she'd never moaned in her safely monogamous life. Every time his freaky monster cock withdrew, she felt like her insides might come out with it.

She had deejayed herself to many an orgasm beneath her husband over the years, but this was incomparable. Her legs were spasming. Her aging knees felt weak. Fluid gushed out of her. *Holy fuck, did I just piss myself?*

Her entire body was flushed. Her shoulder dented the drywall. Her pendulous tits clapped with every impact. She felt like she was being fucked to death. In that mindless sex-blinded moment, she *wanted* to be fucked to death.

She came a second time, nearly ripping his stick off when she slipped and banged against the tank of the toilet, drool hanging from her gaping mouth. Black spots floated in the corners of her vision. Her teeth throbbed in their sockets.

Then she heard a noise that would have been embarrassing if her inner cynic hadn't been fucked into oblivion. The boy was *keening*. His cock felt like it was having a seizure. The floodgates of years of sexual oppression gushed into her trembling body. There wasn't enough space.

She was inflated with the boy's boiling cum. His cock was ejected by the force of its ejaculation. A spritz of jizz sprayed her burgundy asshole like a hot cummy bidet as he fell against the wall. He slumped against the flaking paint, arrhythmically squirting a geyser of sperm.

Sheryl's knees gave, and she fell on the seat of the toilet, hugging it with her thighs for stability. She was being hosed. Cum was skeeting out of his urethra and splashing audibly against her flushed and freckled back. She was doused with seemingly endless pearly ejections from the boy's twitching Mongolian death worm.

She laid her face on the cold lid of the toilet and sighed. Her young friend was hyperventilating as he experienced the sudden return of his faculties. He stood shaking while he witnessed the sloppy wreckage of their post-coital ground zero.

He dressed himself in panic and fled. The door slammed behind him as the milky contents of her boy-battered vagina pooled between her dimpled thighs, spreading across the yellowing plastic lid of the toilet like spilled hobby glue.

That night was something of a breakthrough for Sheryl. She had placed her toe in the waters of the deep and had found them suitable.

She began loitering at the local businesses within walking distance of the campus. She would sit at the coffee shop reading an erotic novel, waiting for some eager beaver freshman to note the provocative cover of her reading material and try to evangelize to her. She would sit on the floor in the philosophy section of the book store reading Nietzsche, waiting for lost sheep. She spent many nights in that first little bar, but she never saw her three-legged choir boy again.

Her increasingly brazen handling of young males caught up with her eventually. She became so used to effortlessly extracting her wants from them that it changed her social habits. These new habits carried over into her delicate blackmailing scheme, where they were far less compatible.

Chapter 48

The End of a Good Run

Sheryl got greedy. She sent another letter. This one informing her cash cow that the demand for dairy had increased. She told them to double their payments, or the police would be made aware of a certain restaurant space (and the activities they could expect to find evidence of within that space). The envelope she sent included color photocopies of all of the incriminating polaroids.

After years of receiving punctual payments, she went against her word: She had been the one that told them the price for her silence would never increase. If she lied about that, what else might she have been lying about?

When Big Man found the letter on the floor of the restaurant, his dormant rage returned with a vengeance. He actually laughed when he read the letter. *What was she thinking?*

The fresh photocopies seemed to hint at an interesting possibility. Maybe she hadn't put Cory's "knickknacks" in the care of a "trusted third party" after all. *She was bluffing all along. She probably has that shit in her house right now.*

Up until this point, paying Sheryl had become like any other tax to Big Man. He had a secretary mail the envelope monthly. He had put the whole thing out of his mind. He would have kept paying her indefinitely, but she had shown her hand: Some old photos of Dillon and Greg. *Big deal.* She had confirmed something he had long suspected but had never been certain enough to act on:

He wasn't in any of the photographs.

Greg had been his best friend. He and Dillon had some okay times together, but it was never the same after Greg died. *I'm going to try to help you out of this mess, Dill, but I'm not gonna try too hard.*

If he could get the kid to let him in the house, he'd tie up the kid, find the shit she had on Dill and leave. If not, he had another plan.

When a reply to her letter failed to materialize, Sheryl thought they were just testing her. Then she read about the fire in the paper. The restaurant was ashes. How could she blackmail them if she had no means of contacting them? She couldn't just text them. She had upgraded devices several times since she had received those threatening texts.

Whoever they were, they had responded to her letter with arson.

She sat in her living room with her dead husband's dirty secrets spread out on the coffee table. She didn't have to pick up Aiden at school for another two hours.

Her threats had been mostly empty, she realized now. She had no interest in going to the police. She didn't want to get dragged into some horrific legal nightmare.

Years ago, when she had first searched his phone, she was still in shock and buried under a layer of prescriptions. She had checked his texts, found only ordinary conversations with her and his coworkers – his contacts list was limited to familiar names. She had checked his photos and saw only pictures of her and Aiden. His browser had been set permanently on private mode. She had tried to get into his email, but it required a password.

Sheryl picked up his phone again. *What do tech-savvy people do when they accidentally delete their photos?* She wondered.

She searched the app store for 'deleted photo recovery.' There were hundreds of results. The description of the most popular result informed her that digital devices don't purge deleted content until users reallocate storage space with new content.

She downloaded the app, waited for the mandatory ad video to finish, and ran the tool. She was disappointed by the results. Many of the recovered images had been of her husband's face just staring into the camera. Some depicted his scalp, probably taken to inspect his hair for bald spots and thinning. She had never realized how vain he was.

Towards the end of her scrolling, there was an image of the smaller guy from the polaroids. His face was red with rage. He was swinging a blurry golf club at the ground, throwing a hissy fit. *Tired of sand traps?*

The last photo was a little more useful. It featured the man from the previous picture with a much larger man. Their outfits looked like golf-themed costumes to her. She used to tease Cory about getting dressed up to golf on a Par 3, but he had insisted that it was considered proper etiquette.

In the photo, they were standing on either side of a beer cart girl. Sheryl looked carefully at the second man. He was massive, and there was something familiar about his face.

Chapter 49

The Stigmata of Aiden Prembach

"So, your mom goes from driving around in a fancy car and going on shopping sprees to impoverished-single-motherville overnight?" Kim asks.

Aiden is suddenly distracted by his vibrating cell phone. He pulls it out of his pocket. The comparatively blinding light from the screen illuminates their little vista in the woods, and before he can answer, Kim grabs his arm in panic and points, "What the fuck is *that*?!"

Aiden directs the light of the vibrating cell phone towards where she points. Two eyes flash yellow, reflecting the light from his phone.

"Yeah, let's not find out," he says, nodding his head towards the passenger door. Kim doesn't need further instruction. She rushes around the car and hops in the truck cab. Aiden hops in and backs out onto the dirt trail, whips the truck around, and drives back to the highway.

"What the *fuck* was that?!" Kim shouts. She is still a little freaked out.

"Probably just a deer or something, but yeah, no bueno," Aiden says as he cracks the window and turns up the air.

"Maybe we should have tried to hunt it. I'm fuckin' starving," Kim jokes.

After a short drive, they pull into the parking lot of a Mexican restaurant that serves food 24/7 out of a window on the side of the building.

"You read my mind," Kim says as her eyes scrutinize a wall of menu items.

Aiden's phone starts vibrating. "I'm sorry. I have to take this. Can you order me the tacos al carbon?" he says and hands her a fifty.

"Yeah, sure," she says before returning her attention to the menu.

She overhears his conversation as he paces back and forth on the side of the cheddar-yellow building, "What's up? ... Yeah, man, no sweat ... better than that reggie your boy was probably robbing you with ... Tonight? ... I don't know man, you'd have to make it worth my while ... Haha, actually yeah, and I'm having like, *romantic* feelings for the lady too ... You serious? Um, yeah, that's enough to justify a little detour ... you want anything from the Taco stand? ... The one across from Mazda dealership ... no worries, more for us ... text me your address. I'll see you in a few minutes."

A pretty Mexican girl slides the window open and asks Kim what she wants. Kim orders in broken Spanish. The girl smiles and hands her the receipt after she rings up the order. Kim sits on the bench.

"Who's calling you at this hour?" she asks Aiden as he approaches.

"Some guy got my number off a dude at your work. He wants me to drop by with a couple of ounces. I was going to tell him to fuck off till tomorrow – not in those words, obviously – but he's willing to pay a stupid amount of money to expedite things. Do you mind eating in my truck?"

"Not if you don't mind picking shredded lettuce from between your seats."

They eat their food while driving down empty streets. They stop at Aiden's apartment complex. Kim waits in the truck. After a few minutes, she sees Aiden descend the stairs, once again wearing a shirt. He opens the door and pulls back his seat, stashes a grocery bag containing a can of coffee, and gets into the truck.

"This guy wants Rain Forest Certified French Roast at this time of night?"

"No, there's a couple of baggies in the can. The coffee is to hide mask the smell if we get pulled over," he tells her.

"You think of everything, don't you?"

"I mostly just think about you bouncing on my balls."

Ten minutes later, they pull into the driveway of a small house with a metal gate around it. It looks like a foreclosure job. The shingles are patchy, and the spreading fungal stain on the stucco wall is visible even in the orange light of the streetlamps.

"You should probably stay in the truck. If this guy hadn't got my number from Frank, we wouldn't even be here."

"No way. If he's a friend of Frank, he's a friend of mine. That guy cracks me up."

Kim crunched behind him along the pebble walkway with bare feet. Aiden texts the buyer, letting him know he's out front. He gets a text back immediately that says the door is unlocked.

The house is a shithole. A dated-looking television is playing a Seinfeld rerun. There is a foldable card table in the middle of the living room. On the table, there is half an Adderall pill next to a razor blade on a CD case.

"Sit down," says a voice from the hallway. Big Man Jr. enters the living room, pointing a handgun with an electric-tape-wrapped cylinder screwed on the end – some kind of DIY silencer. He gestures at the folding chairs around the table. Aiden shrugs at Kim, and they do as they are told. Aiden sets the coffee can on the table next to the CD case.

"Nice whore," Big Man Jr. grunts.

"I feel like this isn't a good way to start a business relationship, friend," Aiden says diplomatically.

"Oh, this *isn't* the 'start' of *our* relationship. I know who you are."

"That makes one of us. The search for one's true self is the work of a lifetime…" Aiden parrots the line from a cartoon he saw on Netflix.

"Shut the fuck up," Big Man Jr. says and points the gun at Kim, "You, cunt. Tape up this chatty fuck to the chair, or I'll rupture an implant," he tosses a roll of duct tape next to Kim's filthy feet.

Kim shoots a terrified expression at Aiden. The playfulness is gone from Aiden's face. He looks tired.

"Bad things happen to mean people, friend," Aiden says in a controlled tone of voice to Big Man Jr., who responds by putting a bullet through the TV set. The silencer is effective. He could kill them both without alerting neighbors (assuming they would even care).

"Tell your cunt to tape you up, or I'll shoot off your tiny penis," threatens Big Man Jr.

"It's actually not that sma… AHH!" Kim is interrupted by another round being discharged, this one nearly hitting her feet. She falls backward in the chair and ends up on the floor. The room smells like moldy carpet and gun smoke.

"Tape your fucking murderer boyfriend to the chair, or the next one goes into his baked potato brain."

"You better do it, Kim," Aiden tells her apologetically.

She begins wrapping him in duct tape.

"Are you shocked to discover your boy here isn't who you thought he was?" Big Man Jr. says, kicking Aiden's chair leg for emphasis, "Did he tell you he was a fucking murderer?"

"He did, actually..." Kim confesses as she wraps another band of tape around Aiden's abdomen. Big Man Jr. hits her in the mouth with the butt of his handgun. She falls onto the floor, raising a shaky hand to her mouth. Her eyes water profusely. She spits out blood and the better part of a front tooth.

"That was a terrible thing to do," Aiden says flatly to Kim's assailant. He is rewarded with similar treatment. The butt of the piece catches him in the cheekbone. His chair tips back from the force of the blow, nearly falling, but Kim jumps to steady it in time. A line of blood drips down her chin onto her cleavage. Big Man Jr. puts his loafer onto her chest and pushes her back on her butt in a seated position against the wall.

"So, this fleck of pig shit told you he murdered my dad then? Did that make you horny, cunt? Did you at least charge him more to fuck you in your diseased shitbox?"

Kim finally reaches her threshold for the night. She is exhausted. Her high is gone. She is crashing from all the carbs she just ate. Her vandalized mouth is in pain. She doesn't give a fuck what this Peter Pan is talking about. She's glad his dad is dead. She hopes his mom sits on a grenade. She leans her head against the wall and zones out.

"Ah, now you're just gonna get all quiet? Just like a bitch would. Yeah, well, he *did* kill my dad."

"Your dad was one fucked up dude," Aiden says in a voice that sounds distant.

"My dad was the best fucking injury attorney in the goddam state!"

"Didn't you ever wonder why Benvolio's burned down?" Aiden asks him.

"My dad said the stove had a gas leak. More importantly, how do you know about Uncle Greg's fucking restaurant?"

"*Fucking* restaurant is right! Did you call your dad's buddy Dillon 'uncle' also? Did he touch your peepee?" Aiden snaps at him without thinking.

Big Man Jr. stares at him in disbelief.

Aiden feels guilty and apologizes, "That was mean, man. I regret saying that last bit. You were probably just a kid…"

Aiden's vision blurs as the bullet penetrates his foot. Blood leaks from the hole in his muddy shoe. He looks up, grimacing, and says, "*Yep*, I deserved that."

Big Man Jr. looks pale. A drop of sweat rolls down his neck into the fabric of his collar.

"My dad's office building had cameras, you evil fuck. You know how many nights I spent staring at a picture of your face?"

"How many nights?" Aiden asks through clenched teeth.

Big Man Jr. stomps on Aiden's wounded food. Aiden starts huffing and puffing like he's in labor.

"Enough to recognize your crackhead little face tattoo and your girly Jesus hair when I saw you come into The B&B tonight," Big Man Jr. spits on the carpet and continues, "You thought you could just mug my old man? My dad worked hard. You wouldn't know about honest work. You saw a guy leaving work on the way home to his family, and you came up on him with your trusty hammer and just bashed his brains in, didn't you?"

"Do you know what was in your dad's briefcase that night?

"How could I? You fucking stole it. Did you just suddenly feel the need to get the inside scoop on the latest fender benders he was litigating?"

"That briefcase had ten thousand dollars in it. It also had a recipe book with a lot of scribbling in it. You ever peek at the notes in the margins of Daddy's recipe book?"

When Kim hears Aiden mention the money, her eyes open. Tired as she is, this part involves her. She had rolled around in that money.

"Ten grand? Was that worth a life to you… a little hooker money for all of your bludgeoning efforts?" Big Man Jr. sits in the folding chairs across from Aiden. He rests his gun hand on the table, pointing the bootleg silencer at Aiden's chest. He looks like he's fighting back tears.

He picks up the remaining half of the Adderall pill and swallows it dry. "The cookbook isn't some big shocker, shithead. My dad enjoyed cooking. Everyone knew that. He said it relaxed him."

"That cookbook is the most fucked up thing I own."

"*You kept it?*" Big Man Jr. asks, trying to keep the emotion out of his voice.

"Yeah, I kept it. If I had known it was you on the phone, I would have brought it. Maybe then we'd be smoking the weed in that can and forgetting all about your fucked-up dad. Instead, we're sitting here acting out the script of some tired-ass crime drama."

Aiden looks down at his aching foot. The carpet beneath it is stained with his blood. "Instead, my foot has a hole in it… Your TV has a hole in it…" he stops talking and twists his neck to check on Kim, "You hanging in there, Kim?" She yawns and shrugs. "Even Kim's teeth have a hole now, man," Aiden says, turning back to look at Big Man Jr.

"I wish you had brought it…" Big Man Jr. says somberly, staring at Aiden with unblinking eyes. "Okay. I give up. What am I missing here?"

"The recipes were modified to better accommodate another type of meat."

"What meat? What the fuck are you talking about?"

"The meat of the children he fucked and tortured in your Uncle Greg's restaurant with Dillon... and my dad."

Chapter 50

Money Problems

Sheryl felt like she recognized the bulky golfer in the recovered photo, but he wasn't in any of the polaroids. This was unnerving. Little weeds of anxiety began springing up through the cracks of her mind's insulating layer of pharmaceutical pavement. She wondered if the big guy had been the one who texted her years ago. She had always assumed it was the third guy in her photos – the chunky mincing one with the mustache.

She went for a drive to kill time before she had to pick up her son. She had taken to listening to FM radio years ago. Back then, her apostasy had opened a world of music to her that she had previously avoided on moral grounds. She knew the devil was the angel of music, and she had always suspected he still did his best work in that industry: oversexed starlets writhing around in leotards, grown men in eyeliner glamorizing substance abuse, smooth-talking drug dealers weaponizing their poetry. She had discovered all the songs everyone else was already sick of, and she was hooked.

She drove past the chapel of the Christian college. She thought she spotted a boy she recognized walking with a group of girls his age. She was like ninety percent sure she had gotten that kid to eat his own semen out of her vagina.

A Billy Idol song was playing on the radio. She stopped using the seek feature and turned it up – *hey little sister, what have you done?*

She drove through a dumpy neighborhood. A dirty child wearing a dented plastic Viking helmet was walking from mailbox to mailbox, pulling out the envelopes and dropping them into a stolen shopping cart. She thought about how this would complicate the lives of numerous people, how their frustration would affect how they treated others, how the way a person is treated forms their worldview, how worldviews affect the way people vote.

She drove past a deteriorating strip mall. On the sidewalk, a gummy-jawed junkie in a statue of liberty costume was gyrating his hips while thrusting a sign for tax services at her Mercedes. She wondered how much they were paying him. She wondered if paying a homeless junkie to wear a sweaty costume in Florida's heat and humidity was predatory or philanthropic. She didn't care.

She felt like she had been driving around for a long time. It would still be a while before she needed to pick up her kid. She parked in the parking lot of a grocery store that had been going out of business for the better part of a decade. She closed her eyes and turned up the music.

Some aging rocker was crooning about the sexual urges he felt towards his neighbor's teenage daughter. The song faded out to a commercial advertising a surgery-free operation that promised to help the listener to achieve a waistline they wouldn't have to be embarrassed about while they lounged at the beach. After the insulting sales pitch, a sexy female voice called out, "Oh, waiter! *I'll have another piña colada!*"

When the next commercial came on, Sheryl stiffened. A booming voice was asking the listener if they've been in a car accident. No? How about a slip and fall? He and his team had years of experience getting people like YOU the money YOU deserve. This little speech was followed by the kind of jingle that makes people kill their pets:

In a car or at the bar, on the floor of the grocery store – if you're hurt and need a hand, call the best, call Curt 'Big Man'.

Sheryl's face went pale. She now knew why the guy in the recovered photo looked so familiar. He was on billboards all over town. She pulled out her phone and googled the name "Big Man."

There he was: Curt "Big Man" Fogelman, Attorney at Law. She retrieved her husband's phone from her purse and held the image that she had found next to a picture of the bulky, suited ambulance chaser. *Holy shit.*

That afternoon on the drive home, Sheryl gave Aiden another stranger-danger lecture. She told him never to open the door for *anyone* – not even the police. She told him the world was a wicked place. She told him there were evil men that liked to cut little boys' penises with scissors. Aiden cringed in the seat next to her.

That evening in her room, she unboxed and set up an expensive laptop that she had bought when it came out but never used. The house had Wi-Fi because Aiden said his games required it. A dialogue box said she needed to enter a network key. She clicked a small question mark in the corner of it. Another dialogue box said she could find the key on the bottom of the modem.

The modem was in the kitchen. She had argued about its placement, but Aiden had said that was the only place with a jack. She left her room and photographed the bottom of the modem. Once back in her room, she zoomed in on the network key and copied the cryptic looking sequence of alphanumeric characters into the box. It worked. She was online.

She scoured social networking for Curt "Big Man" Fogelman, Attorney at Law. He didn't have a Facebook account, but his wife did, and she wasn't just a casual user; if her son so much as sneezed, there was some loaded status update about it.

There was photo after photo of "Dins from Hubby," too. Years ago, looking at pictures of nice dinners a husband cooked for their wife might have stirred up a little jealousy in Sheryl. She would have pushed away the feeling by reminding herself of the scriptural role of a Christian wife. Then she would pity the couple for being so lost.

She scrolled through the woman's timeline until she found what she was looking for: a photograph documenting a surprise birthday for Big Man featuring lots of friends and family. Everyone with a profile was tagged in the photo, including a mischievous looking little shrew with a lot of gel in a little hair.

His name was Dillon Melbobby, and he was standing next to Big Man's son with an arm wrapped around the boy's shoulders. This was the man carrying a dead kid's torso in the polaroid she had. Dillon's page was private, but at least she had found his name. She saved everything of interest in a folder on her desktop.

It didn't take her long to find Big Man's website. His email was listed on the contact page. She knew these guys already knew her name and address, so she just logged into the email address she had to make when she bought her phone and started typing.

She sent the following email:

Hi Curt or maybe I should address you as "Big Man",

Your payment is due in three days. A man as successful as yourself should have no trouble covering the cost of my raise.

I saw what happened to the restaurant. I hope that wasn't intended as a threat. Mr. Dillon Melbobby will receive a visit from uniformed men soon if things don't go my way.

Sincerely,

Sheryl Prembach

Two days passed. She was out riding a theology major's crying face when it happened. Big Man had tried to get at her son. Posing as a pizza man seemed to be his way of saying *the kitchen may have exploded, lady, but grandma still knows all the recipes by heart.*

She told Aiden to go to his room and lock the door. She tried to dope herself with Clonazepam, but it only transformed her fear into guilt. She had to go to the police. She put her husband's stash in her purse next to the gun and left the townhouse. Before she could start the Benz, her phone made a single ding noise. She had a new email. A feeling of dread descended on her as she read the message.

Dear Mrs. Prembach,

Thank you for contacting our firm. I think there has been some misunderstanding. You referenced receiving a raise (congratulations, by the way) in your email, but I had our girl run a search for your name in the payroll system, and we have no record of your employment.

I found the remainder of your email somewhat distressing. The acquaintance of mine that you seem to be referencing was found dead this afternoon. Someone set flame to his mobile home.

You seem to have predicted this in your email with your "visit from uniformed men" comment. How did you know this was going to happen?

Initially, I thought your reference to "the restaurant" seemed like a non sequitur, but then I recalled that a restaurant burned down recently that used to be owned by an old family friend that seems to have dropped off the face of the earth. I only remembered the article because reading it had reminded me how much I still miss him.

I'm confused. Mrs. Prembach, are you threatening to burn down my business? Were you somehow involved in the death of my acquaintance, Mr. Melbobby?

Please feel free to stop by our office and discuss this with me in person. I would hate for a simple mix-up to get you into the kind of legal trouble an email like the one you sent me could precipitate.

Always fighting for you,

Curt "Big Man" Fogelman, Attorney at Law

Sheryl had taken a gamble. She had gone all-in on a seemingly flawless hand only to be told the game was Go Fish. She had cut open a chicken that shat gold eggs and found only blood.

What the fuck do I do now? She sat in the Mercedes, chewing her nails.

She had grown complacent in their arrangement. Her personal tragedy had been more than enough; she didn't need life's mundane obligations too. As a married woman, she had done plenty of work but not the kind that fills out a resume.

There was something else too. She sincerely believed that she was going to burn in a lake of fire for all eternity. A mind that exists in this reality struggles to take things like 'stocking shelves' and 'store walk-throughs' from the 'district manager' seriously. She wasn't going to spend her time in hell's waiting room slaving for the daily denarius.

She needed to cut their overhead in a hurry. She drove to a dealership and sold her car for cash. She used a fraction of that money to buy basic transportation at the dealership across the street. The car she bought had been in an accident, but the damage had been strictly cosmetic.

Shepherding off college boys into darker pastures had given her an uncommon familiarity with the area's motels. She negotiated with the landlord at one of the least expensive of them by agreeing to pay in advance on a month by month basis – most of his customers paid by the hour.

She was exhausted, but she couldn't risk staying in that townhouse another night. She stopped at a gas station and bought one of the large colorful cans that promised teenagers endless energy. She read the label. *Holy shit, this stuff is poison.* She drained the can on her way to the hardware store. She loaded up on cardboard boxes and sped home to her son.

She scanned the parking lot carefully before emerging from the dinged-up Saturn. After the car was packed with what little she could fit and Aiden was strapped in beside her, she drove through a calm residential area to confirm that she wasn't being followed. Satisfied, she headed for the motel.

The next morning, she took an Uber to the townhouse. She dialed the number on one of the many corrugated plastic street signs that read, "We Pay Ca$h for *ANY* House." The buyer got a great deal in exchange for making the transaction as easy and quick as legally possible. Sheryl even threw in the furniture.

Chapter 51

Aiden's Worst Memory

Aiden and his mother had grown even further apart over the years, which was a real accomplishment given the size of the motel room they lived in together. She was rarely around.

She had told him the motel was temporary. This wasn't entirely untrue; it was temporary for him.

In the early years following his father's death, he assumed his mother's transformation had been due to grief. As he aged, he increasingly blamed her medication. Despite the adverse changes in her character, he still loved her. She was his mom. He just felt more comfortable when she wasn't around – he would carry guilt about this sentiment far into his adulthood.

One night, his mother came home drunk, smelling of something he couldn't identify. She turned off the TV hooked up to his PlayStation. She told him to shut up when he protested.

A woman cried on the other side of the deteriorating wall, but that wasn't unusual. Their neighbors changed several times a day. They all had one thing in common: a complete lack of concern about how much noise they made.

His mom had sat on the springy twin bed opposite his, staring at him with a look he would remember for the rest of his life – she was deflated, hollow.

"Aiden, you're old enough to know that I've been fucking the landlord."

Aiden fondly recalled a time when his mother wouldn't have said that word even if you'd paid her. *Who was this broken woman?*

When he didn't respond, she continued, "The house money is gone. It has been for a while."

He remained silent.

"Your mother isn't a prostitute."

He had no words.

"Dennis and I started fucking years go. He knows our situation. He's a good guy, that Dennis," she said this last bit in a way that sounded as if she was talking to herself.

Aiden knew Dennis was the landlord because the man had come in a few times over the years to spray for bugs, replace air filters, etc.

"Hasn't gotten a dime of rent from us for a couple of years now. I think he was just too embarrassed to bring it up," she stood and walked to the window. She peered through the tiny gap between the antiquated floral curtains. "Well, he brought it up tonight."

Years of living there had given Aiden grit. He had adapted. He shoplifted from the shitty grocery store during the summer when he no longer had access to school lunches. He had taken to hanging out in parking lots and smoking cigarettes with other teens that lived in the area. He had tried weed for the first time behind a dumpster with a kid named Chris, whose older brother grew the stuff. He had gotten close to another kid one summer only to never see him again after someone sold his mom fentanyl instead of oxy.

He had quickly learned from the lives of his peers that life could always get worse. His mom seemed to be announcing that it just did. His heart sank.

"Aiden, I can't do this anymore," she told him, speaking from somewhere in the muffled depths of her despair.

"Can't do what, Mom? What are you talking about?" Aiden was scared by her words and embarrassed by her drunkenness.

"I'm sorry. I just can't cut it anymore. I'm tired of being afraid. I'm tired of the bottomless empty chore of this *'gift'* we've been *'given.'*" Sheryl tilted her head back and looked up at the water-stained ceiling of their room. She hissed in a cracked voice, "You can have it back, Lord!"

Her son didn't say anything. He didn't know what to say. A part of his mind thought she was just wasted and wished she would just pass out like usual. The other part was trying not to feel the weight of her confession.

"Aiden. Your mommy loved you," her eyes had taken on a glassy quality. She walked into the bathroom. In movies, when a character discharges a firearm indoors, they play a loud noise, and everyone goes on dropping one-liners. When Sheryl pulled the trigger, the sound was earthshaking. It sounded like the whole world just cracked in two; to the sixteen-year-old boy on the bed, it felt like it had.

Chapter 52

Big Man Jr. Learns the Truth

[...]

"I don't even want to be called 'Big Man Jr.' anymore," their former captor turned impromptu therapy patient says through yet another bout of sobbing. "People always said it sounded dumb, but *he* used to call me that… I wanted to be just like him!"

"What *is* your name anyway?" Kim finds herself asking this question for the second time in one night. She sits in the passenger seat, wincing as she wiggles the protruding remnant of her broken front tooth with her fingertips, trying to free it from her bloody gums.

"Tim," he responds, wiping his tears on the padded shoulders of his cheap suit.

"Let it out, buddy. I still cry sometimes about my parents too. It's like, cathartic, or whatever," Aiden says in the back seat, as he sprinkles some of the weed from the coffee can into a folded rolling paper. The three of them are in Tim's shitty sedan, heading to McDonald's.

"I just feel like such an idiot," Tim says, slapping the steering wheel with his palm when he says the word 'idiot.'

"I feel you, man," Aiden says and then licks the line of adhesive and rolls the paper, pinching the joint in places to even out the distribution of its contents. "I grew up thinking my dad was a victim, too. Thought he was just a hard-working guy that got ground down by the world. The suicide note he left made it sound like he was wrestling with mental issues…" he lights the joint, passes it to Tim behind the wheel.

"Part of me is just wondering whether me and my mom ate… you know… pieces of someone's kid. I mean, my dad cooked all the fucking time," Tim says as he reaches over to pass the smoldering joint to Kim.

"GOT IT!" Kim says. She lifts a bloody shaking hand from her mouth. In her bloody fingers, she holds the loose remnant of the tooth she finally extracted. She drops it out the crack of the window and wipes her fingers on a T-shirt Aiden lent her back at his place. She notices Tim's hand offering the joint and takes it. "I still can't believe the two of you shady motherfuckers were raised by a couple of kiddy fucking baby eaters," she says indelicately, laughing at the sheer fucked-upness of it all. She takes a sip of the Red Bull from Aiden's apartment and then rolls down the window further to spit blood.

"I'm really sorry about your tooth…" Tim says for the billionth time.

"You should be, you jerk," she snaps, but it doesn't sound convincing. She just wants some French fries right now.

The sun is creeping up behind a horizon of silhouetted strip malls, power-lines, and palm trees. The sky is a magnificent vaporscape of pinks and purples. Tooth or no tooth, she feels lucky to be alive.

Tim wasn't a villain. He was just fucked up and sad. When he had first seen the security video of Aiden bashing his dad's brains in with a hammer, he had vowed, *someday I'm going to find that guy and shoot him in the face.*

But back at his house, Tim had done something genuinely heroic: He had suspended confidence in his sense of being right long enough to hear another person express their perspective.

Aiden's claims had been shocking, but he didn't have the face of a liar. Something about his complete lack of guilt had eaten at Tim's resolve. Tim had begun to feel like the bad guy. He had hit a girl in the face – broke her tooth. He was supposed to be avenging his father's death, but it hadn't felt right. He had severely injured two people in his own living room, and his conscience was acutely aware of it.

Aiden had told him everything. Elements of his story triggered flashes of memory in Tim's mind. He began to see his dad as the person Aiden was describing. He remembered thinking it was strange how his dad had shown no emotional distress over the tragic death of Dillon, his supposed lifelong friend. He remembered hearing the name 'Cory' in conversations his dad had on the phone. He remembered his dad getting defensive when his mom had questioned him about the finances.

Tim had begrudgingly agreed to let Kim drive the three of them in his car to Aiden's apartment. He wanted to see the evidence with his own eyes. He sat in the backseat, keeping the gun fixed on Aiden, but deep down, he already knew the guy was telling the truth. His stomach was in knots when they entered the apartment.

Aiden had shown him everything his mom had collected on his father, "Uncle Greg," Dillon, and her own husband. Tim was in shock. He just sat on the loveseat, shaking his head, repeating, "I can't believe this shit."

When he thumbed through the cookbook, full of his dad's handwriting detailing cannibal-friendly modifications to the recipes in the margins, he fucking lost it. He spent almost an hour in Aiden's bathroom. He cried, barfed, and cried some more. His dad had been his role model. Now he was a revolting embarrassment – worse, he was a fucking monster.

Tim's mom had divorced his dad a couple of years before his death. She told Tim that they had just fallen out of love, but he wondered if there hadn't been more to the story. She moved out of state. She hadn't even stayed in touch with her Tim, the same kid she had gushed about on Facebook ad nauseam. She had always seemed so social online, but after the divorce, she deleted everything. It was like she had evaporated. Tim had taken it really hard.

After his dad died, he felt like he was alone in the world. Family members had assisted with organizing the funeral, but they hadn't helped him out financially. His dad hadn't left a will. The bank owned pretty much everything.

His dad's business partner felt bad for him, so he hired him to make copies, do data entry, etc. – he was basically the office's bitch. Tim worked hard, but without a degree, he wasn't going anywhere.

If he had discovered all of this shit on his own, it probably would have been too much for him – he might have even pulled a Sheryl – but Aiden knew what he was going through, and commiseration is powerful stuff.

Aiden had seen a photo of his dad putting his dick in a dead guy's mouth. He had been under the same roof as his mom when she painted the bathroom with her own brains. Yet, here he was puffing on fatties with a big-tittied stripper. If this Jesusy looking deadbeat could pull through, so could Tim.

"I think I want some nuggets too," Kim says, as Tim pulled into the parking lot of McDonald's.

Chapter 53

Mary Takes a Phone Call

Mary wakes up on Arthur's sofa. The living room smells toxic, but Mary has gone nose-blind to the corpsey stench.

Memories from the previous day trickle into his mind slowly. He remembers rolling the joint and then not smoking it. He pats around on the floor. He finds it next to a bloody shard of glass. *Today is going to be a good day.*

He walks into the kitchen and turns a knob on the oven. The gas catches, and a ring of blue flame hisses beneath the spiral burner. He tucks a loose strand of pink hair behind his ear, leans in, and lights the joint. He turns off the burner and pulls on the joint.

Fuckin' brand new day. A blank slate. Infinite possibilities.

Mary smells his armpit. *Yikes.* He forgot to put on deodorant before his little adventure last night. He finds a stick of woman's deodorant in a bathroom drawer. He sets down the joint on the edge of the counter and applies liberally. He thinks for a moment and then pulls down his sweatpants, grabs his sack, and runs the deodorant along the hairless skin between his asshole and his balls.

He finishes the joint and flushes the roach. He brushes his teeth with Arthur's toothbrush, gargles with Arthur's mouthwash, and then hits himself with one of Arthur's four colognes. The bottle says, *Cool Water.* He wonders how many women associate this fragrance with waking up dumped on the side of the road.

Someone should sell a fragrance called Rohypnol, he thinks. *The commercial could be like, "Rohypnol, a fragrance for 'them'" and then show a bulb-nosed jock with a punch-me face grunting above the camera like he's having a hump.*

Mary looks in the mirror. Tom looks back at him. He sniffs the cologne on his teddy bear shirt a second time and furrows his brow. *Weird, this stuff is kind of growing on me.*

He rifles through the scant selection of makeup Arthur's wife left behind. He applies mascara to his lashes. He rolls on some sparkly watermelon lip balm. *I bet this shit is made of Bambi hooves,* he thinks, while smacking his lips. He has a faint bruise on his cheekbone from one of Arthur's love slaps, but unfortunately, the wife's concealer isn't even close to his shade.

Arthur's phone starts to buzz. The notification screen says sixteen unread text messages and two missed calls. He picks up the phone and tries not to sound like he's wearing mascara. "Hello?" he says as he walks into the living room.

"Good morning, this is Sherriff Alfie Dawson attempting to get in touch with a Mr. Arthur Reed. Are you Mr. Reed?"

Mary's heart beats faster. *Dang, way to kill my buzz, copper.*

"This is he," Mary says with Tom's voice.

"I'm sorry to disturb you this early in the morning, but your neighbor, a Ms. Megan Reinhard, is facing some fairly serious charges, and she mentioned you in her testimony…"

Mary's palms get clammy.

"Megan? *Shit.* I'm sorry, *shoot*. What happened to Megan, Mr. uh…?"

A trickle of sweat rolls between Mary's should blades.

"Dawson, Sheriff Dawson. Listen, Mr. Reed, I'm not at liberty to discuss the details of the case at length, but during her testimony, your name did come up…"

Mary unconsciously pokes at Arthur's earlobe with his toe while he searches for the right thing to say.

"Yes, Sir. We did talk last night," he finally manages.

"I realize that given your marital status, this situation calls for a bit of discretion."

"I appreciate that, Sir," Mary says, trying to hide the excitement from his voice.

"It is a gentlemen's obligation to respect the privacy of another man's affairs when possible. In this case, Ms. Reinhard herself, although not without a few harsh words, has stated clearly on record that you were not present during the incident. The evidence we have collected thus far seems to make this clear."

Relief washes over Mary like cool water.

"I hope she's okay. Is there anything I can do to help?"

"There *is* actually. During her testimony, Mr. Reinhard described a person that... Uh, you seem to have discussed with her in a series of text messages exchanged prior to the incident."

"I did?"

"The uh, *person* in question is described as, among other things, male – possibly wearing a, uh, skirt... You mentioned seeing this person hanging around the park?"

"Oh yeah, I did see someone that meets that description."

"We were hoping you might remember some additional details about this person ...distinguishing tattoos, prominent facial features, skin color, and the like. We are trying to draw up a quick composite to pass on to the uh, media. Would it be possible for you to pay us a little visit at the station today?"

Mary feels a little dizzy. He sits down on Arthur's chest and collects himself. *Here goes nothing.*

"I'd love to, Sheriff, but I only seen this queer once, and I wasn't paying much attention. I saw a skirt on a gentleman in my peripheral vision, and I was about done looking at that mess, if you take my meaning."

"I do, son. Well, sorry to disturb you. Don't hesitate to drop in on us if any other details come to mind. We sure would appreciate it."

"If I think of anything else, I will do that, Sir."

"Thank you for your time, Mr. Reed. You have a nice day."

"You do the same, Mr. Sheriff."

Mary ends the call and leaps up from his seat on Arthur's chest and dances jubilantly. The relief is torrential. He was terrified that he was going to have to leave before his novelty blender showed up.

Holy shit. I'm going to blend *EVERYTHING*.

Chapter 54

Mary Makes a Phone Call

Mary consolidates his stolen pot and papers in a plastic baggie from the kitchen. He finds a duffel bag full of shoes in the bedroom closet. He dumps the shoes out on the floor and organizes them in the closet by color. He carefully picks up the gun off the floor and examines it. He locates the safety and switches it on. He wraps it in his soiled girl costume and puts it into the duffel bag next to his balled up ruffle socks and his pink Velcro shoes. He zips the weed into an interior side pocket.

He walks down a hallway he had intentionally been avoiding. Kids' rooms always make him feel weird. He peeks into what must be Dale's room. The kid's bed is shaped like a plastic car. *Fucking hell, my bed was shaped like a bed!*

He peeks into Presha's room. He starts crying. Through the blur of his tears, he can just make out a hair straightener on the edge of a vanity that was painted pink with chalk paint and decorated with sparky bubble stickers of smiling cartoon deserts.

He sniffles as he grabs the straightener and runs back out of the room. Outside of the girl's lovingly decorated room, his emotions subside. He returns to the duffle bag in the parents' bedroom and tucks the straightener in the duffle bag next to the gun.

He checks the delivery status of his orders on Arthur's phone. His packages have been picked up from the facility and are out for delivery. This cheers him up a little.

He finds cleaning products beneath the sink in the bathroom and paper towels in the kitchen. He scrutinizes the hair clipper charging next to the sink. He wonders if Arthur used it to trim his nether hedges. Then he remembers Arthur's gnarly bush exfoliating his nose while he swallowed the man's dick. *Yeah, this is probably just for young Dale's sporty little fade jobs,* he decides.

Mary looks in the mirror at his long pink hair. *Eh, this alt chick thing is a little played out anyway,* he thinks, trying to console himself. He doesn't believe it, though. *Alt chicks will always be sexy, no matter what shit music they pretend to like – the end.*

He prays, *may I be the kind of girl that looks hot with a shaved head.* He carefully shaves his head over the toilet and flushes it all away. He runs his head under the shower, dries it off with a paper towel, and flushes that too. He looks in the mirror. His makeup is a little smeared, but he looks kind of kinky. *Not completely terrible,* he decides.

He begins the arduous task of spraying and wiping down everything that came in contact with his body. Mary isn't a naturally paranoid person, but talking to the policeman on the phone had been a little intense. He may be innocent of Arthur's death, but the situation doesn't look good, and the sheriff doesn't sound like the kind of guy that makes a habit of giving cross-dressing squatters the benefit of the doubt.

As Mary cleans, he fantasizes about being a housewife. He is making everything perfect for his hubby. As he scrubs the tub, he gets lost in a fantasy of being on his death bed from cancer caused by a life of cleaning hubby's house with noxious chemicals. He imagines his dream husband bringing his bald ass some sorry flowers and introducing him to his replacement: A *real* woman. *Fuck, this fantasy sucks.*

After cleaning the bathroom, he polishes Arthur's dead knob and balls a second time, this time with bleach instead of slobber. He always thought death boners were permanent, but Arthur's has begun its final descent. *Yucky.*

Mary has entertained many elaborate fantasies about prison, but he isn't dumb. He knows that in reality, it would be more violent than sexual. If the inmates didn't kill him, tray after tray of inedible bologna and 3D printed cheese sandwiches would. He shudders.

The doorbell rings. Mary freezes in place. Then he hears the sound of a large truck pulling away and realizes it was just the FedEx guy. *Yay, it's like Christmas morning!*

He does one last sweep of the house and finds the shattered remains of the dropped plate of boiling blueberry pie. *Shit, this stuff is like glue,* he thinks as he meticulously picks dried purple glaze from the grout of the tile with a paper towel covered fingernail. *I'm definitely going to need a manicure.*

He puts everything back where he found it. The exploded bedroom mirror he murdered would just have to remain a mystery. *Maybe the cops will think the skirted stranger couldn't cope with his own sexually confused reflection.*

He peeks out the peephole to check for neighbors – none. *Everyone is probably inside masturbating to midget porn,* he thinks cynically. He opens the door, retrieves the two boxes, and brings them in the house.

He fishes his phone out of his purse and calls Gwen. He gets her voicemail. *Dang.* He *really* doesn't want to make the next call, but he needs a ride and can't think of anyone else. He met the creep on craigslist years ago. Mary doesn't hate sitting on his cock once in a while, but the guy has some serious emotional baggage. He finds the name in his contacts and hits dial.

Chapter 55

Love and Friendship

Kim, Aiden, and Tim are sitting on a curb in the McDonald's parking lot, stuffing their stoned face with fast food.

Kim's tooth socket throbs, but she is so baked she barely feels the pain. She wanted French fries, but they had already switched to their breakfast menu. The hash brown she was chewing was surprisingly compatible with the salty taste of blood in her mouth.

Aiden bites into an egg sandwich. The hole in his foot ached. Earlier, when Tim was puking and crying about his cannibal dad in the bathroom, Aiden had sat on his kitchen counter and washed the wound, poured peroxide in it, and bound it up. It hurt, but his occupation didn't come with healthcare. He figured if his leg started turning black, he'd limp into an ER and work out the financial end of things later.

After Tim finishes his food, he picks up a flattened half-smoked cigarette someone discarded on the pavement. Kim looks at him with an eyebrow raised and then fishes into her bra for a lighter and hands it to him. He thanks her and lights up, taking a deep drag and exhaling tobacco smoke into the humid morning air.

"Hey, I know you guys are sick of hearing it, but I just want to apologize again. I'm so sorry about tonight. I said some *horrible* shit back there, and I treated you both *so* unkindly," he takes another drag and continues, "but even though tonight sucked, I'm still happy we met. I've been really, *really* lonely. Acting like a fucking prick has not helped me make friends," Tim says, in a voice modulated with emotion.

"You're okay, bud. I'll be your friend," Aiden offers, patting him on the back reassuringly.

"So long as we don't have to call you 'Big Man Jr.' anymore. Holy crap, that shit was so dumb," Kim says after swallowing a mouthful of bloody egg.

"We?" Aiden smiled at Kim. He felt happy that she had unwittingly referred to them as a pair.

"Huh. I guess I did say 'we'..."

"So, are *we* like, a couple now?" Aiden asks, blasting her with his most potent shit-eating grin.

She spits blood on the ground and turns to him, "Here's how it's going to go, piss boy. I'm going to get fat sucking orange soda through my new straw-hole because fuck a dental implant," she pushes the bloody tip of her tongue at him through the gap in her teeth. "Then I'm going to lay around in sweatpants all day on your sofa next to *this* trigger-happy motherfucker..." she pokes Tim a little too hard in the ribs, "...smoking up all your fuckin' weed and playing your stupid video games on that big ass TV."

Tim is smiling. Living the victim story and fantasizing about revenge all the time had been eroding his soul. Sitting on a curb, eating garbage next to these kinky dorks is warming his heart. The way they were so quick to forgive him after what he did to them is reauthoring his cynical notions about humanity. It occurs to him that all he ever needed to feel joy in this life was friendship... and maybe love? His thoughts drift to a girl he hasn't seen in over a month. She is the only person willing to toss him the occasional pity fuck in his disgusting house. In doing so, she had unwittingly kept him human.

They crash at Kim's place because it's the closest. The three of them pass out on her gigantic bed. Several hours later, they are awoken abruptly by the sound of Judas Priest blaring from somewhere in the room. *BREAKIN' THE LAW! BREAKIN' THE LAW!*

It's Tim's ringtone.

"Uh, sorry guys," he rubs his eyes and takes a moment to register where he is and who is with. Kim rolls on her side and reaches for the bowl and grinder on her bedside table. Aiden yawns and examines his bandaged foot. Tim looks down at the caller ID and thinks, *today is the first day of the rest of my life*. The caller ID say "Cumslut Mary."

He looks at the other two mischievously, puts the phone on speaker, and says, "Hey Mary, I missed you."

A male voice on the other end of the line says, "Junior, I need a ride." Kim and Aiden exchange looks, their grogginess is replaced immediately by curiosity.

"You know I'm always good for a ride, little lady," Tim says and gives Aiden a wink.

"No, not that kind of ride… I mean sure, that's fine too, but I need an *actual* ride. Like, in your car. Fucking Gwen isn't picking up her phone, and I'm at some dead guy's house with a new blender. This thing can blend ANYTHING," something about the cadence of the voice speaking sounds vaguely familiar to Aiden, but he can't place it.

"Wait, is he talking about the one from the infomercial?" Kim cuts in.

"*She*," Tim gives Kim a look that says, *just go along with it, trust me*.

"Sorry, is *she* talking about the one from the infomercial?"

"Who was *that*?" the voice demands.

"That's my friend Kim."

"You have friends now? Are you fucking her?" the voice sounds a little jealous.

"No! I mean, yes, I have friends now, but—"

"I mean, it would be okay if you were, I guess, but—"

"No, I'm not fucking anyone, Mary!"

"Whatever, man. Listen, you're not going to believe this shit. This fucking blender turned a remote control into *powder* – batteries and all! I fucking flushed a remote control down the toilet!"

Tim covers the phone's mic with his hand and whispers, *"Roadtrip?"*

Kim and Aiden nod their heads vigorously.

"Text me your address, baby, and we'll be there as soon as we can."

Epilogue

Xena is adopted from Animal Care and Control by a nice Canadian couple on vacation.

Mary doesn't get in trouble.

A Note From The Author

Hi,

Thank you for reading this book.

If you enjoyed it, please leave a positive review. It only takes a few seconds, but it means a lot to me.

Love,

Matt

Made in the USA
Monee, IL
22 November 2020

48942364R00121